The Gutter Chronicles

About the Author

David A. Todd is a civil engineer by profession, and a writer by passion. His interests include history (especially American history), politics, and genealogy. He writes novels in multiple genres, non-fiction books in USA history, poetry, and Bible studies. A native Rhode Islander, he has lived in Kansas City, Saudi Arabia, North Carolina, Kuwait, and Arkansas since 1991.

His engineering career has been in consulting civil engineering, primarily in public infrastructure. He had written articles for six different print publications and three on line publications on the subject of infrastructure, flood control, and construction contracting.

Items available by David A. Todd

Fiction – Short Stories
The following stories deal with teenage grief at the loss of a parent.
>"Mom's Letter"
>"Too Old To Play"
>"Kicking Stones"

The following short stories feature Sharon Williams Fonseca as an unconventional CIA agent.
>"Whiskey, Zebra, Tango"
>"Charley Delta Delta"

Fiction – Novels

Doctor Luke's Assistant, a church history novel (1st Century)

In Front of Fifty Thousand Screaming People, Mafia influence in baseball

Operation Lotus Sunday, a novel in China

[July 2014] *Headshots*, the sequel to *In Front of Fifty Thousand Screaming People*

Non-fiction

Documenting America: Lessons from the United States' Historical Documents

A homeschool edition of Documenting America

The Candy Store Generation: How the Baby Boomers are Screwing Up America

"The Learning Curve: 11 Suggestions for Accelerating Your Professional Development"

Thomas Carlyle's Edinburgh Encyclopedia Articles [Editor]

The Gutter Chronicles
The Continuing Saga of Norman D Gutter, Engineer

Volume 1

Including
An excerpt from
The Collected Poems of
Norman D. Gutter

David A. Todd

2012

Dan,
I hope you enjoy this,
David Todd

THE GUTTER CHRONICLES
The continuing saga of Norman D. Gutter, Engineer
Volume 1

Copyright 2012 by
David A. Todd

Cover by David A. Todd

THE GUTTER CHRONICLES
The continuing saga of Norman D. Gutter, Engineer
Volume 1

TABLE OF CONTENTS

THE GUTTER CHRONICLES
The continuing saga of Norman D. Gutter, Engineer

Chapter 1
The Interview

It was a cold day, but that was to be expected for January 2nd. A strong easterly wind howled along Main Street between the three-story buildings on either side as a young man uncertainly approached his destination on foot. The building was non-descript, sort of like the man himself: building with brick front, small hanging sign that creaked in the wind, sidewalk clear of the frozen stuff but stained with signs of recent rock salt use; man of average height, average build, no outstanding features, dressed for business but with obviously inexpensive clothes, no jewelry, anxious eyes. Looking through the glass front he saw a small but attractive lobby. There was a certain bustle, as a couple of men and women crisscrossed the area, holding papers and seeming to be in a hurry. Down the hall he could see an older man and woman talking. At the entrance door were two women and a man smoking, hanging close to the door to stay out of the wind and cold as much as possible.

"Well, here I go," he thought. As he neared the door the smokers parted. They all avoided eye contact with the man and with each other. With his eyes down, a can filled with crushed butts served as a focus of his attention. Inside he approached a receptionist behind a counter. She was about to speak to him when the phone rang and she took a call. He waited perhaps ten seconds as she talked to the caller, tried an extension, and then paged an individual, finally saying, "Good morning, may I help you?"

"Yes please, ma'am. Norman Gutter here for a job interview at 10 a.m. with Mrs. Mize."

She advised him to have a seat while his party was sought. It took barely a minute before a tall, slender woman approached him and introduced herself and tried to put him at ease.

"Hello Mr. Gutter. I'm Minnie Mize. Welcome to I.C.E. Engineering. Did you bring this cold weather with you today?"

She handed him a job application form, just a bit different than the one he had mailed in with his resume, and said he should fill this out. Twenty minutes later he was ushered into a small conference room. Mrs. Mize said she was Human Resources director and that she would conduct the interview. A couple of other people would sit in, she said, and perhaps would have some questions for him. A tour of the offices would ensue, followed by lunch and a brief follow-up meeting for him to ask questions, after which they would have him on his way to the airport by 2:30 or so.

They chatted a bit. "So, I'm curious. If you don't mind my asking, what kind of a name is 'Gutter'?"

"It's originally German, ma'am, Gütterman. My great-grandfather immigrated here in 1914. His boat landed just after the outbreak of World War 1. At Ellis Island he decided his name sounded too German, so he shortened it to Gutter."

People started coming into the room—an older man, followed by two young men, and a woman. What happened next was a blur—Norman would have been hard pressed to recount this to anyone. The door was closed and his interviewers introduced themselves, in rapid fire succession. Mrs. Mize had barely started the interview when a phone in the room beeped loudly, a page was made, and one of the men got up and left. As he did, two more men entered and had seats but were not introduced. One of them was wearing a navy blue jogging suit with light blue stripes and tennis shoes, his jacket unzipped, revealing a sweat-soaked tee shirt. He had an unlit cigarette in his hand, which he tapped constantly on the palm of his other hand. He didn't speak at all. The interviewers said they would ask a few questions not only about his college studies and summer employment, but also about some of his earlier life experiences. Then the questions began to come at him fast and furious.

"What is your earliest childhood memory?"
"How did your parents treat you as you were growing up?"
"Do you play softball?"
"Or basketball?"
"Are you willing to travel?"
"Tell us about the 'C' you got in this course."
"How did you like that summer surveying job?"
"What are your main career goals?"

And many more, on and on. Norman felt terribly uneasy and uncomfortable, and wondered if the interview procedures had been patterned after an FBI grilling that someone saw in a movie. The room got hot, but no one turned on the ceiling fan.

The phone continued to interrupt and blurt out names and line numbers, but no one turned down the speaker. People came and went without rhyme or reason or introduction.

Finally, as if by a signal that Norman missed, the interview was over. He was left in the company of a man for the tour—was it Jimmy Bob? Or maybe John Rob? From floor to floor and building to building Jimmy, or John, introduced him to every person they came in contact with, mentioned department names and functions, took time to chat with a couple of guys about some sports event for that night. Norman was sure he even got introduced to the janitor somewhere on the tour.

About noon they donned coats, left the main building and walked about two blocks to a small café on the downtown square. They went through the ordering line, selected burgers and fries from the limited menu board, and had seats in a booth. So much, Norman thought, for the advice of his college advisor: take all the interview flights you can; at least you'll get a free trip and a nice lunch out of it. They were soon joined by a couple of others, a man and a woman, who had been in the interview. Norman hoped he would not be required to remember their names, as he might as well call them Adam and Eve. The conversation floated between sports, the company, cars, the food, and the weather. To Norman it was all still a blur. He had not expected to be interviewed by committee. The noise in the cafe seemed deafening. The people in his party were constantly being greeted by other diners. The food was greasy, but tasty. Norman was glad when they got up, bussed their table and exited back into the cold.

Back at the office, Mrs. Mize gave Norman some information about I.C.E. benefits, which he spent some time reading. She came back and answered his questions about the benefits package. They seemed okay to him. Minnie then said that the "head man" wanted to meet him briefly, and would be available shortly. Would he mind waiting? Shortly turned out to be a forty-five minute wait in the lobby. He read the I.C.E. marketing brochures spread out on the table. He scanned a booklet by the Chamber of Commerce about the city, Appleville. But mostly he watched the continuous flow of people through the lobby and down the hall. The receptionist was almost never off the phone. People constantly went in and out the front door, usually carrying papers, books, or rolls of drawings. Federal Express and Airborne packages began to pile up on the lobby table. This place certainly seemed to be busy, and the people seemed happy, if a bit stressed. He began to drift off to sleep.

Finally Mrs. Mize came back and escorted him to a row of offices, where he was introduced to Jim Main. Norman didn't quite get his exact title, perhaps President or Chief Operating Officer, but he understood him to be in charge. Clean cut, younger looking than expected, with office walls decorated with diplomas and licenses and photos of projects, Mr. Main seemed to be just what he, Norman Gutter, as he started his career, was hoping to become. Main gave him a few kind words and said he hoped he wasn't overwhelmed by the interview process. Norman lied and said that it went fine. Main talked about his plans for the company, which included expansion into new markets, new regions, and perhaps overseas engineering, and said how he needed good, young engineers to accomplish this. He asked if Norman had any question that hadn't been answered.

"Yes, what does I.C.E. stand for?"

Jim Main smiled and simply said, "Nothing, any more. At one time it may have stood for something, but no one can remember what it is."

With that, the interview was over. Minnie gave him a check for his trip expenses. She told him to expect a letter in a few days, but that she was optimistic he would be offered, and she hoped he would accept.

Norman left the building. Despite the strong sunlight, the chilled wind blew colder than ever. He paused on the sidewalk, just far enough away from the smokers to avoid the second-hand smoke. What should he do if they offered? It seemed like a good company, and growing. If he took a job with them he would probably be secure at least long enough to get his professional engineering license. But things seemed strange. He was a bit uncertain. And how would he be able to tell his parents, "I've taken a job at ICE Engineering"? The kids at school wouldn't stop the polar jokes after he told them where he was interviewing.

Well, no point in worrying about it till he got the letter. He walked the half block to where he had left his rental car. Neatly tucked under the windshield wiper was a small envelope. Norman read, "You have been over-parked. If this is your first offense, place $10 in the envelope and...." Only then did he notice the two hour parking signs.

It was indeed a cold day.

Chapter 2
The First Day

It was ten minutes before 8:00 a.m., on a Monday morning, when Norman Gutter next approached that same doorway. No smokers greeted him this time, and the cigarette butt can was gone—well, not entirely, as he could see it down the sidewalk a ways. Two rolled up newspapers were against the building where the can had been. He thought he could still see a trace of the salt staining, but maybe not. Certainly the place looked different to him on this warm May morning.

A letter had come a few days after his interview, just as Mrs. Mize had said. It did contain an offer, not as much as he hoped for, but not too bad. Included were some brochures from the local Chamber of Commerce, explaining how cheap it was to live in Appleville. Norman had scheduled other interviews, and he received three other offers. Despite the unusual interview process, he had seen something in I.C.E. Engineering that he liked. It seemed to him that this was a company on the move. They were hiring people and opening branch offices. They were turning down work, because they couldn't hire people fast enough to do it. The management seemed young and progressive. And so he had turned down the other offers, all of which were for more money in larger cities, and to I.C.E. he would go.

It was a new receptionist who greeted him. In a heavy southern accent she said, "Have a seat, Mistuh Guttah, and Mrs. Maize will be with you soon."

There was none of the bustle today that he had noted at his last visit. In fact, the place seemed almost like a tomb. No one was in the wide hallway leading back to the offices. The phones were not ringing at all. No one rushed through the lobby or came in the front door. Norman attributed it to the time of day. But 8:00 gave way to 8:15, and still there was no increase in activity. The receptionist handled a few calls. Once he heard her say, "Mistah Justice is in a meeting right now. May ah take a message?" When she wasn't on the phone, her head was down while she flipped through a mail-order catalogue.

Finally, about 8:25 a.m., he saw people in the hallway. All at once about fifteen people walked in his direction. He recognized some of them from his previous trip. As they reached the lobby they scattered in different directions. They all paid him no mind.

It was only a minute before Minnie Mize came up to him and said, "Welcome again, Norman. Come back to my office and we'll get all the employment forms filled out."

The paperwork took about forty-five minutes. There certainly were a lot of forms. Minnie worked at other things while he sat across the desk from her and completed the forms. At last he was finished, and the human resources director said, "All right, Norman. Let's get you to Ned Justice. He's going to be your first supervisor."

She led him just down the hall to an office near hers, which turned out to be empty. "Well, I guess he's out smoking."

To the back door they went, but there was no one there. "Well, maybe he's down at the café getting a cup of coffee."

So they walked the same two blocks he had walked on his interview and entered the same café as before. A few customers were drinking coffee, but apparently he was not there, for Minnie said, "Well, I guess I don't know where he is. Let's check back at his office."

They reversed course, came to the same office as before, but still no one was there. "Mr. Gutter, I'll let you sit in my office while I try to track down Ned. Hopefully we've just missed him."

Norman sat there for a few minutes before he heard that southern voice make a page over the loudspeaker in the hallway. "Naed Juhstice, diahl 201; Naed Juhstice, diahl 201." Minnie was in her office a split second later.

"We ought to be able to track him down now," she said. But her phone did not ring. Not right away, and not for five minutes. She had gone back to her work while waiting for the call, and Norman just sat there.

At last Minnie said, "Well, it seems that Ned has disappeared without telling anyone. That's actually not too unusual. Let me get you a copy of our employee manual and our technical standards. Until Ned shows up, I'll just sit you in the conference room and let you read up on those. Ned should be here shortly. He may have been between buildings and not heard his page."

So they went down to the conference room. She gave him three medium sized notebooks, and left. Norman started reading the employee manual first. It contained a series of personnel policies. They were boring to read, the sort of thing you need but you hope you don't ever have to read. He found the policy on "Flex-time" amusing: "Normal office hours are 8:00 a.m. to 5:00 p.m., with one hour reserved for lunch at the employee's preferred time. We do allow flex time, however. If you need to come in fifteen minutes late one day, just make it up at another time." That was it. That was the whole policy. Norman didn't know if it was a joke inserted into the manual, or if the flex-time policy was that you could come in fifteen minutes late. He'd have to check that one out.

The policy on sexual harassment had obviously been written by a lawyer, he thought. There were plenty of legal terms. The words "him" and "her" never appeared except in the format "him/her". At the bottom of the fourth and last page he saw something someone had written in by hand before the photocopy was made: "Don't screw around on the job." He wondered if Mrs. Mize knew that someone had done this to her master document. Except for that, there was nothing to take note of. Norman soon dozed off.

"Sleeping on the job on your first day, huh? You'll fit right in here."

Norman quickly awoke and saw a tall man towering over him, at least 6 feet 4. He was dressed in a purple jogging suit, with the jacket open, revealing a sweat soaked tee-shirt. His hair, what there was of it, was combed straight back but was wind blown. He was wearing what appeared to be cross-training shoes. He smelled of cigarette smoke. As they shook hands, Norman could see the other man's watch—it was 11:15 a.m.

"Hi. I'm Ned Justice. Sorry to keep you waiting. I forgot that you were starting today. Minnie should have reminded me on Friday. After my morning meetings I left for a work-out, and just got back. Did anyone tell you that we have an all-company meeting every Monday at 7:30? Don't tell Mr. Luzano that I didn't tell you. Let's go to my office."

Down the hall they went. Ned never stopped talking as they walked or as they took seats in his office. Norman realized that his man had been part of the interview team, but had never been introduced to him, nor had he asked a question. They were in his office less than one minute when his phone buzzed, and the receptionist told him he had a call.

"Excuse, me, but this is important." Ned talked for at least ten minutes. During that time, a woman came into his office and presented some checks for him to sign, which he did without looking at them. Right after that a young man came into his office with some letters to sign, which he again did without looking at them.

Right after Ned hung up the phone, it again buzzed. "Mistuh Justice, William Moore is heah in the lobby to see you."

"Sorry about this, Norm, but I've got to go see him, and it's going to take a while. Why don't you go get lunch, and we'll meet back here about one o'clock and get you going on some work."

With that, Ned Justice quickly went out and Norman was alone in his office. The desk was immaculate; not a piece of paper on it. The shelves were neatly lined with books and pictures and plaques and diplomas. One was from a civic organization, which read: "To Ned O. Justice, with appreciation for service on the Board of Directors".

Norman walked the now-familiar two blocks to the café, but found it full and a long line waiting to place orders. Across the street was a grocery store in which he found a small deli. He bought a newspaper to read while eating his chicken sandwich. The headline was in large, bold type, the sort that was normally reserved to announce a war or something of that gravity: **MAYOR INDICTED FOR CORRUPTION**. It seemed that the mayor of Appleville, Dave Tuggle, was accused of having city street department crews install a swimming pool, fencing, and driveway at a new house he was building. An investigation by the sheriff's department had determined this had a commercial value of $35,000, making the mayor's alleged action a felony. Other stories included statements of support from various members of the community, including Ned Justice, he noticed. Others were calling for the mayor to resign, rather than have the city be put through the trauma of a trial.

Back at the office, Norman did not find Ned Justice right away. Waiting in his office, he saw that a copy of the company newsletter had been placed on the empty desk, and so picked it up to read it. Right at that moment Ned Justice walked in.

"Still here, Norm? Did you get some lunch? Go ahead and take that newsletter—it never says anything of great importance anyway."

He allowed Norman no time to answer. Ned began immediately to describe a couple of projects Norman would work on. One was a storm sewer extension project in the city of Appleville; the other was a sewage lift station for a commercial development in the city of Nepgip, a twenty minute drive. "You'll like working in Nepgip," said Ned. "They've got some great restaurants down there."

Getting lined out on these projects took the better part of the afternoon, as Ned Justice proved to be a busy man. Between phone calls and visitors and smoking breaks, Norman had as much time sitting by himself, reading correspondence and waiting, as he did of actual contact with Ned. They looked at engineering drawings and files, and Ned said something about needing to bill the clients right away, as accounting was screaming for the billing worksheets.

As 4:30 neared, Norman could tell that Ned seemed to be bringing their time to a conclusion. He stood at his desk, pulled out a cigarette, put on his jogging suit jacket, took a step around his desk and toward the door and said, "Okay, Norman, it's late enough now, why don't we just complete this tomorrow." He must have sensed Norman's confusion, for he stopped and said, "Any questions?"

"Well, yes. Where will my desk be?"

"Oh, I completely forgot. Let's get you situated."

Out of the building they went, into and across the alley to one of the other buildings, as Ned said, "We're going to sit you next to Peter Pan to start off with."

Norman suppressed a laugh at that, as he thought Ned must surely be joking about that name. Upstairs they went, to a small room with two work stations and space for a third. A man sat behind one desk working on the computer, while another desk obviously had an occupant who was not present at the moment. Ned made the introduction.

"Norman Gutter, meet Peter Pan." They shook hands. Peter had a gleam in his eye, knowing that Norman thought surely that couldn't be his real name and wanted to ask him about it, but dared not on their first meeting.

"Norman, here's where you will sit," said Ned, pointing at the empty space in the room. "Someone dropped the ball in not getting your desk and computer here before you got here. Sorry about that. Why not just sit at Joe's desk here for a couple of days. He's out of town until Wednesday."

Norman couldn't believe it. They had known he was coming since January, and known the exact date for a month now, and yet they were not ready for him. What had he gotten himself into?

Chapter 3
The Hazing

So Norman D. Gutter began his engineering career at a borrowed desk, with a gadfly supervisor, and a concern that he had made a terrible mistake. The second day at work didn't turn out much better. In his mail slot he received a computer user name and password from the IT Department, but saw no activity as far as bringing his own work station in.

Peter Pan was cordial to him, but seemed extremely busy and had little time for small talk or making him feel welcome. Ned Justice breezed through about 10 a.m. in a blue jogging suit with the jacket unzipped, revealing a sweat soaked tee-shirt, gave him a computer manual to read, said he would see him mid-afternoon and get him going for real on one of the projects, and was gone as quickly as he came. Minnie Mize called him to say that the Accounting Department needed him to come down and fill out some payroll forms, but they were very busy at the moment with month-end closing and would be calling him.

Lunch hour found him at the same deli as the day before. Minnie Mize was also eating there with a man and a woman, but ignored Norman except for a nod of recognition. As he ate, Norman wrote a letter to his dad, trying to say positive things but having a difficult time finding them.

When he returned to his desk, or rather Joe's desk, three other men were at Peter Pan's area, talking quietly with him.

There on the desk was a phone message for him: "NG – call Mr. Lyon," and gave an outside number. His first message! Who the man was, or what he wanted, was unimportant. He dialed the number, and a woman with a pleasant voice answered.

"Appleville Exotic Animal Rescue Center."

"Yes, may I speak with Mr. Lyon, please."

After a couple of seconds, the nice voice on the other end exploded in anger. After some vulgarity, she said, "I'm tired of these crank calls and I'm going to the police about this. Five calls in ten minutes is way out of line." SLAM.

Norman stared at the telephone for a moment with a puzzled look, then realized he had been had. At about the same time the other men in the room burst out laughing. Anger quickly welled up within him, but it passed and with a little effort he laughed too. The four of them had a few minutes poking fun at Norman. This broke up when one of the print room guys came upstairs, lugging a computer, and put it on the floor where Norman's desk should be.

*   *   *   *   *

Arriving at work the next day, Norman found Joe returned to the office, and the few things he had left on his desk unceremoniously stacked on his computer, still inanimate on the floor as it had been when he left the day before. Joe was curt, almost surly in his greeting. With no place to work, Norman went looking for Justice to see about a work station. But Ned was no where to be found. Mrs. Mize sympathized with his plight, and said she would make some kind of temporary arrangement. Within thirty minutes a 5-foot layout table arrived, together with a folding chair. Still no desk, but it was a start.

That morning Norman spent time working on his storm sewer project. He got as far as he could without having to use the computer for CAD work. A call to the IT manager resulted in a promise to get his computer up and running right after lunch. He arrived promptly at 1 p.m. and introduced himself. Peter Pan chimed in, "Just call him 'Data'—everyone else does." Data made a vile reply, then got to work setting up the computer. Downloading software from the network, arranging for printer and plotter access, giving instructions to Norman, etc., took the better part of three hours. A network outage in another building caused the longest interruption, though there were frequent pages, "Data, call…." Finally he was up and running, and he had Data's promise that he would have a telephone within a day. Right at quitting time Ned Justice showed up, wearing a red jogging suit with the jacket open, revealing a sweat soaked tee-shirt, and said that they would meet tomorrow afternoon to review the storm sewer drawings. He should have them plotted by 2 p.m. Norman failed to notice the knowing glances exchanged between Ned, Joe, and Peter.

*　　*　　*　　*　　*

Thursday dawned dark and cloudy, with a fine mist falling and thunderstorms threatening. Norman arrived early, planning to complete his drawing and plotting well before the afternoon meeting. Calling up the drawing, he found it was in an older CAD program that the current network software did not support for remote plotting. Seeking a way to convert the drawing to the new CAD program, Norman could find no easy way to do so. Peter Pan, also in early for a change, told him that I.C.E. had failed to purchase the conversion module of the new software, and that the only way to do it was to go into the list of elements in the CAD database and convert them one line at a time, using three specific keystrokes followed by hitting the space bar to go to the next line. Norman was concerned, as there were thousands of lines in that database. He set about this ridiculous task, which he figured would eat up an hour or two of his limited time. He was hard at it when Joe showed up at 8 o'clock with a surly look on his face.

Tap-tap-tap-thud. Tap-tap-tap-thud. Tap-tap-tap-thud. Joe listened to three minutes of this before saying in an aggravated tone, "What the devil are you doing?"

"Converting this old drawing to the new CAD version so that I can finish it and plot it."

"Well, use the program, stupid."

Norman ignored the insult. "Peter said I.C.E. doesn't have it."

"Well, he's stupid too. I just used it myself last week."

"When did we get it?" Peter Pan asked.

"We've had it for about four months, but it's not on the network; you need the diskette."

CRASH. A huge thunderclap shook the building.

"Fine," said Norman, "I'll call Data and get the diskette."

"No, no, no, you idiot," Joe growled. "It's a bootleg copy. If Data knows we have we'll lose it. Foreman's got it."

"Who?"

"Al Foreman. You know—old man, sits in the basement of the main building. He's the senior designer. Didn't you meet him?"

"Sure. I thought he wasn't computer literate."

"He's not, but he keeps the diskette. Just go over and see him and get it."

"Okay." Norman started to leave, then stopped. "What exactly do I ask Foreman for?"

Joe picked up the phone as he answered. "Just ask him for the CAD-Con diskette. And for goodness sake, don't go telling Data."

Foreman's work area had to be the most cluttered in the company. Piles of papers were stacked on desk, table, floor—everywhere. Magazines and books were stuffed into every portion of his shelves, and on top of the shelves. Rolls of drawings, yellowing with age, were scattered everywhere. Foreman sat at his drafting table, talking on the phone. It appeared he had been editing what looked to be a company standard.

"Good morning, Al."

"Good morning. I'd rather you call me Foreman. And you're …?"

"Norman Gutter." They shook hands.

"What can I do for you, Gutter?"

"Joe sent me over to you to get the CAD-Con diskette."

"Oh, got a drawing to convert, have you? Alright, but I have checked out the diskette to someone. Hang on just a second."

Foreman rummaged around on his drafting table for a couple of minutes. "Well, that was right here yesterday," he said. He shifted to his desk, continuing to mutter softly. "Where is it? Stupid folder. Come on, come on," and the like. Norman stood there, the minutes ticking off in his head and the cost to the time he didn't have to work on his drawing. Foreman shifted from the desk to a table, then checked various papers on his shelves, then started going through his piles. He interrupted his looking to get a cup of coffee.

"It can't take much longer," he said, plopping in his chair and grabbing a pile off the floor. Norman glanced at his watch. Twelve minutes so far.

"Are you in a hurry?"

"Well, I have a 2 o'clock deadline I'm trying to make."

"Oh, no problem. Once I find the folder where I log who I gave the diskette to you'll have it in five minutes."

Ten minutes later and the search was over. "Ah ha! You little duker, you." Foreman acted like a schoolboy who had just found a dollar on the playground. The folder was marked "Top Secret", and had lined sheets inside with rows and rows of names. All except the last one had been crossed out.

"Okay, here it is. I gave that to Herb about a week ago, and he never gave it back. I suppose I should have followed up on it. Do you know where Herb sits? No? Across the alley in the basement of Building 2. Chew him out for me for not returning the disc."

Norman headed out. At the side door the rain was just starting in earnest. Regretting not checking the weather that morning and bringing a rain jacket, he made a quick dash across the alley to the building he sat in, but went down stairs instead of up and was at Herb's desk not more than thirty seconds after he had left Foreman. Herb was just hanging up the phone as Norman walked up.

"Herb. Hi I don't know if you remember meeting me earlier. I'm Norman Gutter."

"Hi Norm," Herb said cheerily. "What can I do for you?"

"I need the CAD-Con diskette from you."

"I don't have it."

"Foreman has it checked out to you."

"That senile old coot. I gave it back to him on Monday."

Back into the rain and across the alley went Norman. Foreman was not at his desk. He searched the basement, then the first floor, asking everyone he saw if they had seen Foreman. He finally saw him come in the front door, dripping wet with a bag of donuts in hand. "Foreman. Herb says he gave you back that diskette three days ago."

"Oh, no, I forgot to log it in again. Worse than that, I forgot to log it out, 'cause I don't have it. C'mon, let's see if we can find out who has it."

Back at his desk, Foreman first got another cup of coffee, then had to shake off and hang up his raincoat. He took a copy of the company phone directory and scanned it. "I remember now. I gave it to Walter in survey. He ought to be in the office on a day like this. Why not go see him and get it for me."

Norman was only too happy to expedite the retrieval of the missing diskette. Upstairs and to the front door he went, stopping under the canopy, where today the smokers were sticking close to the door. Traffic on Main Street was very crowded, though flowing. He had a choice to wait for a break in traffic and rush across the four lanes, or go out in the pouring rain to the crosswalk and pedestrian call light. Thinking of his tight schedule forced him to choose the latter. In the Survey Department he found Walter, who said Foreman had never given him any diskette. Better call him and find out who he really gave it to. Norman used Walter's phone, but got Foreman's voice mail.

He reversed his course through driving rain and found Foreman again at the coffee pot. It was now 9:30.

"Well, if Herb gave it back and I didn't give it to Walter, who the blazes did I give it to? It must be someone in survey." The phone list was again consulted and a new name selected—Louise in survey—so back Norman went. With this street crossing, Norman was completely soaked. Louise didn't have the diskette either—Foreman had never given it to her. A call to Foreman again went directly to voice mail, and so Norman made his fourth crossing of Main Street that day, with it still raining hard. This time Foreman was in the rest room when he got there.

Years later, Norman could look back on this episode and laugh, but it was not funny that morning, as he dealt with the older man who had lost the bootleg diskette, and sent Norman out into the rain time and time again to go to this or that building to check with another person. Always there was a surprised denial, a statement that Foreman was losing it, and a voice mail mail at the other end of the line. An hour and a half thus passed, with Norman back again at Foreman's desk.

"Gutter, I'm sorry, but I just don't know who else I might have given it to." The phone list was searched, and Foreman stopped and thought for a moment. "You know, I was talking with Ned Justice about this earlier this week, about trying to get a legal copy of the program. I don't believe I would have given him the disk…but I don't know anyone else who might have it. Why don't you check with him? If he doesn't have it or know who does, I'll have to say it's lost." Upstairs to executive row was but a few seconds for the running Norman, but Ned wasn't in his office. Did he expect anything else? A ten minute search of all buildings failed to turn up Ned. But then, from an upstairs window, Norman saw him pull into the parking lot and head toward the back door of the main building, wearing a gray jogging suit with the jacket partly unzipped, revealing a sweat soaked tee-shirt. Norman caught up with him at the back door as he was smoking there.

"Ned, Foreman says that you might have the CAD-Con diskette."

Ned took a puff. "He gave it to me yesterday. Do you need it?"

"Absolutely. I have to convert the storm sewer drawing before I can make the changes and plot it for our meeting."

"I gave it to Data this morning."

"You what? Isn't that a bootleg copy?"

"Oh, I know. I worked it out with Data. He's going to load it on the server now and order the real program right away. That way we will only be using the illegal copy for a few more days. There's almost no risk and we really benefit."

Norman turned to go into the building and find the IT manager. Ned turned toward the street and said, "Two o'clock, right?"

Norman found Data where he always was, at his desk, watching four monitors and tapping at a keyboard.

"Data, have your loaded the CAD-Con program onto the network yet?"

Data was distracted, and seemed not to have heard it all. "The CAD-what program?"

"The CAD-Con program. Ned Justice says he gave you the diskette this morning."

"I don't know what you're talking about."

"You know, the CAD-Con program. The one that converts drawings to the new CAD program. Foreman has a bootleg copy of it and loans it out to people. Ned says he gave it to you this morning to load on the network while we are waiting on the licensed copy. I've got to convert a drawing in the next," he looked at his watch, "two hours and I really need it. If it's not on the network yet could I at least borrow the…"

Data had stood up and stared at Norman. "A bootleg copy, you say? We don't have *any* illegal software on the network. Ned Justice better not be starting that again." He was agitated and upset.

"Now don't get sore at me. I just came to you because Ned said…." Norman suddenly stopped. For the first time that morning he realized he had been had again. It was all a hoax. There was no CAD-Con program or diskette. Joe and Foreman. Maybe Ned? And how many others?

Data didn't seem to be in on the gag. "Alright, tell me again what this is, and how is Foreman involved? He doesn't even use the computer."

But Norman turned and rushed out of the room, angry at those who had done this to him and angrier at himself for having fallen for it for over three hours.

*　　*　　*　　*　　*

Tap-tap-tap-thud. Tap-tap-tap-thud. Norman worked through the noon hour, almost frantic to get the drawing converted and get ready for the meeting. At 1 p.m. he didn't look up when Peter Pan and Joe came back from lunch, and they wisely didn't say anything to him. Tap-tap-tap-thud. Tap-tap-tap-thud. Joe made no complaint this time. About 1:30 the drawing was converted, and Norman made a call to Justice and left a voice mail saying that he would be a bit late for their meeting. At 2:15 the drawing came off the plotter. A minute later he was at Ned's office which, as usual, was unoccupied. Right about that time the page came over the phone speaker, "Norman Gutter, Ned Justice on line five. Norman line five." He picked it up.

"Norman, I need to cancel our meeting. Something has come up at a job site that I need to handle. Let's meet tomorrow morning whenever you get in." There was a bit too much levity in Ned's voice, and Norman realized he was probably the ring-leader. He hung up without reply.

He went up front to check his mail slot. The new receptionist, a sweet lady named Gayle, said, "Oh, Norman, you just missed a call while you were on the phone with Mr. Justice." She handed him a slip of paper: "Please Call Robin at …."

Gayle looked shocked as he wadded up the paper and threw it at her. He figured the number was probably for the State Aviary.

Chapter 4
J.J. Weast

"Norman, this is J.J. Weast from the Accounting Department."

Norman moved the receiver away from his ear and stared at the phone. Never in his life had he heard a voice like that. Was it a man's or a woman's? It was deep and gravelly, and could easily been either. How do I answer, he thought. I can't say Mr. or Ms.

"Yes…J.J.?"

"Norman, I hope Minnie has talked to you about coming down to Accounting to fill out a form or two. We have to get your W-4 and your benefits withholding forms filled out before we run payroll this week. I would hate to have to withhold your check just for lack of a signature."

"I agree with you on that. Shall I come right down and fill them out?"

"No, I've got them partially laid out, but have misplaced your folder. Give me about fifteen minutes to get it out and then come down and see me."

Good, thought Norman. In a quarter hour I will solve the mystery of J.J.'s gender.

* * * * *

At the appointed time, Norman opened the door to the Accounting Department and walked in to meet with the raspy-throated J.J. At the six or seven desks in the room were men and women busy at work. There were no nameplates anywhere, and no one looked up to find out what he wanted. He saw one desk with no one at it in the back corner, and went to it, but could not tell who sat there. Finally he blurted out, "It this J.J.'s desk?"

Without looking away from her computer screen, a woman said, "Yes, that's where J.J. sits."

Norman looked around for the normal signs one would find at a work station to tell if it belonged to either a man or a woman, but he found none. There was no purse, no sports posters, no real decorations of any kind. A framed photograph showed a family group of a man and women and three teen-age children, but which one was J.J. —the father or the mother? It was an average height and size desk, with a typical office chair—not the type a secretary would have, but rather one with arm rests. The bookshelves contained mainly notebooks, full of official I.C.E. accounting documents, no doubt. He saw there were two personal books, motivational types. The work area was fairly neat, but not perfectly neat. Of course, Norman told himself, neatness is not strictly a male or female trait, though usually it was stronger in the latter.

A sheet of paper on the desk was a to do list, one item being, "Call NDG & have him fill out forms". The handwriting was neat, but again, how can you tell if a man or a woman wrote it? Finally he turned away from the desk to the woman who had answered him before and said, "I was supposed to meet with J.J.

now. Where is…"—he wanted to say 'he' or 'she'—"Is J.J. here?"

"J.J. had to leave unexpectedly. A large check came in this morning's mail that had to go to the bank right away. Are you Mr. Gutter?"

"Yes." He noticed that even this co-worker of J.J. Weast had not given him the pronoun he needed.

"J.J. left me your folder. The forms should be in here."

Five minutes was all it took to fill out the simple forms, and Norman was on his way out of the building and back to his desk. On this short walk, he scrutinized the two people who passed him, heading in the general direction of the Accounting Department, but of course could not tell if either of them, a man and a woman, were J.J.

Back at his desk, he wanted to ask Peter Pan if J.J. was a man or a woman, but he figured he would look stupid doing so. As for asking Joe, well, after the hazing incident, they hadn't exchanged a dozen words.

Toward mid-afternoon, a check of his e-mail revealed an announcement about the monthly all-company meeting, to be held the following Monday. It would be hosted by the Accounting Department. *Good*, thought Norman. *They'll probably call everybody up and introduce them, and I'll find out who J.J. Weast is.*

*   *   *   *   *

Norman did not spend his weekend troubled over this, but it crossed his mind a time or two. Writing a letter to his dad, he included the following comments.

"The folks at ICE have been pretty good to me. They are all friendly, save one. They sure have strange names, though! The guy who sits closest to me is called Peter Pan—even has a name plate that says that. I assume it's a nick name, but have no clue as to what his real name is, and haven't worked up to asking him yet. Another "person" is J.J. Weast. I have spoken with him/her on the phone, but can't, from the voice, tell if it is a man or woman. I should meet him/her at the all company meeting tomorrow, and so the mystery will be solved."

*   *   *   *   *

Monday found Norman at the office a full half hour before the start of the meeting. He got coffee, and a doughnut from the box, and had a seat. Chairs were still being set up by men and women, some of whom he recognized from his visit to Accounting. At last the meeting started. The Accounting Department head, a woman named Donna, opened the meeting by describing the duties of the department. She then began to call out the department members by name and had them come up to the front. Norman waited anxiously as one by one they, people he recognized already, stood in front of the company. What would J.J. be? He finally decided it must be a woman. "The telltale signs point more to a woman than to a man. Yep, she's gonna be a woman," he said softly under his breath. Six had been called up when Donna said, "And J.J. Weast is our other member. J.J. is in the branch office this week, working on shutting down their accounting system and transferring all the data back here."

Norman could not believe it. He knew nothing more about J.J. Weast now than at that first call. He had to find out who J.J. was, and whether he was, or she was, a man or a woman.

*   *   *   *   *

The week following, Norman made it a habit of passing by the Accounting Department as often as he could. Usually the door was closed, and of course he would not open it just to see who was at J.J.'s desk. On those occasions when he was passing by and the door was not closed, he always seemed to be prevented from seeing all the way to J.J.'s desk. Or, once, he could see the desk but there was no one there. When ever he saw anyone from the Accounting department in the halls in the company of another person, it was always a person he recognized. Was he ever going to learn J.J.'s gender?!

Finally, Norman took what was for him a very bold step. Mid-morning one Friday, he phoned J.J.'s extension, and soon found himself in J.J.'s voice mail.

"J.J., this is Norman Gutter. J.J., I was looking for someone to have lunch with me today, and seeing how we have never actually met, I thought it would be a good opportunity to get acquainted. Please give me a call and let me know if you are interested."

It was less than a minute when he got a call back. "Hi Norman. J.J. Weast here. Lunch is an excellent idea. Why don't you come by my office about 12:30 and we'll go then. I like to eat a bit late."

With that, Norman went to his weekly department meeting. At 12:30 promptly, he was at the Accounting department and entered. Everyone was gone, to lunch no doubt. And there was no one at J.J.'s desk. Thinking that the missing J.J. would appear momentarily, Norman sat in the chair at the desk. He leaned back, then spied the note, carefully placed in the middle of the organized desk.

Norman,

I felt sick to my stomach about 11:30, and have left for the day. I left you a voice mail, but decided to leave this note in case you came by here before checking your messages. I'll call you next week and we'll get together one day.

J.J.

Foiled again, Norman thought. He began to think that the gender of J.J. Weast, like the name of Peter Pan, was one of the secrets of I.C.E. that he would never learn. He decided to give up trying—though not completely, as the future will tell.

The Legend of J.J. Weast
By Norman D. Gutter

He wanders daily in the halls.
She places many inside calls.
Can anyone for certain say
"I know the one they call J.J."

That gravel voice is hard to place.
A guy or gal—I've seen no face.
Tell, is it beauty or the beast?
What is the sex of J.J. Weast?

Should I seek to meet her...or him?
What kind of e-mail do I send...her?
Words so sweet, or "Let's hit the gym"?
But first I must learn J.J.'s gender.

I speak to her upon the phone
it seems once every other day.
He must always eat lunch alone,
this phantom worker named J.J.

Accounting now is where she sits,
before that, some big money lender.
A him, or her, or just an it?
No one I know knows J.J.'s gender.

I searched and searched till I was ill.
Of such pursuits I've had my fill
Success? I've had none in the least
in my long search for J.J. Weast.

I wander by Accounting's door,
but what I see does just perplex.
Will I be asking ever more
"Is J.J. my or the other sex?"

We scheduled lunch for twelve or so,
but then he or she didn't show.
I feel just like a sheep that's fleeced
expecting to meet J.J. Weast.

His photo no one's ever seen;
her painting none will ever render.
Was it homecoming king or queen?
Please SOMEONE tell me J.J.'s gender!

At last I was in such a stew,
this question I asked all I knew:
"Will I, when my work days have ceased,
have learned the sex of J.J. Weast?"

Look at his desk; she's never there
I don't think he is anywhere.
I looked each hour, each working day
but never saw that one, J.J.

I must admit I've got it bad,
like my head's caught firm in a blender.
I think I'll go stark raving mad
if I don't find out J.J.'s gender.

To office, lunchroom, parking lot,
at first I walk, and then I trot.
I've searched this firm from west to east
but haven't yet seen J.J. Weast.

When creativity takes hold
I'll come up with a plan that's bold.
In some sly and ingenious way,
I will restrain and catch J.J.

This clever plan, what should it be?
A trap? A snare? An evil hex?
What must I do to some day see
the secret of this J.J.'s sex?

It seems I must at last confess
to pastor, rabbi, or a priest,
for daily now I do obsess
about the sex of J.J. Weast.

But what should I be looking for?
A man who's fat? A gal who's slender?
I always miss, then try once more
to discover J.J.'s gender.

If some day I would have success
and get out of this gender mess,
I'd shout at a gigantic feast,
"Now hear the sex of J.J. Weast!"

I hired a good Private D.,
although that made me a big spender.
He charged a grand, then said to me,
"I couldn't find out J.J.'s gender."

I started this as a young man,
but now I've grown both old and gray.
I walked at times, but mostly ran
in my pursuit of old J.J.

So I advise each one who's new:
"There's one thing that you must eschew.
You'd as well catch a pig that's greased
as learn the sex of J.J. Weast."

And when at last my work is done
I will affirm complete surrender.
It drove me mad, yet was great fun.
I never did learn J.J.'s gender.

Chapter 5
The Strong Arm of the Regulator

Approximately two weeks after Norman started working at I.C.E., Ned Justice informed him that they had a meeting with the City of Appleville to discuss the storm sewer extension project. The project was for a developer, but the storm sewer would be owned by the City after construction, so they had regulatory authority over it, and had to approve it before construction started.

"I don't like having to review this with them, but there's no way out. I sent them the drawings early in the week, and they want to meet about it. Be prepared to go there with me tomorrow morning about 10."

With that Ned was gone, in his gray and white jogging suit, an unlit cigarette hanging from his mouth. Norman got the project file and checked the drawings, correspondence, and the calculations. He felt that the drawings were not very complete, at least not compared to the ones he had used as examples. Had he known the project was being submitted to the city, he would have preferred to take a bit more time to bring them to a higher state of completion.

*　　*　　*　　*　　*

The next day was swelteringly hot, as can happen during June in Appleville. No breeze eased his discomfort as Norman walked from the municipal parking lot to the office. His work area was hot and humid when he arrived. Both Peter Pan and Joe were not there that day, which was unfortunate, as he wanted to ask them what to expect in the meeting with the City. He knew they had both recently completed projects in Appleville.

At ten minutes before ten o'clock he was in Ned Justice's office, but Ned wasn't there. A quick pass through the main building didn't result in his finding him. At the reception area, he asked the new receptionist, a very young woman named Priscilla, if she had seen him.

"No sir, Mr. Gutter. I don't believe Ned has arrived yet today."

Norman waited at the back door of the building, which is where he usually found Ned smoking. About five minutes after 10, Ned rounded the corner, wearing a sea-green jogging suit with the jacket unzipped, revealing a sweat soaked tee shirt, walking from the direction of the café, reading a newspaper as he walked, with the ever-present cigarette dangling. Even on this day, with a scheduled meeting, Ned was casually dressed.

"Good, I'm glad you're here, Gutter," said Ned as he tossed his cigarette butt into the street. "Let me get my folder and we'll head right out."

They walked the two blocks to city hall, Ned with his folder and Norman with the project files, arriving about fifteen minutes after their appointment. The receptionist immediately ushered them back to a conference room in the old building, where a middle-aged man was seated, reviewing the drawings. Ned made the introductions.

"Norman, this is Chowdahead, city engineer. Chowdahead, this is Norman Gutter, our newest engineer."

They shook hands. Norman could not believe the name. Chowdahead? Surely this was a joke. The two older men looked quite serious, however. Perhaps a nickname, or a foreign name poorly transliterated into English and horribly pronounced. Norman noted that it was not 'Mr. Chowdahead,' nor was it said as if it were a first name. It must be a nickname, he decided. It was obvious that Chowdahead did not appreciate being kept waiting by someone who had but a short distance to go to get to an appointment on time.

"Let's make this brief, shall we?" Chowdahead started off. "These drawings are not acceptable. They lack sufficient detail to construct the project, and don't really give me enough information to make a proper review. The calculations, however, are acceptable, except for a few items I've noted."

Ned took the calculations and handed them immediately to Norman. He scanned them as Ned and Chowdahead discussed the drawings. He saw that the marks were all editing marks—spelling corrections and clarifications of page titles—rather than engineering comments. *Boy, this guy is sure picky*, he thought. What difference does it make if I spelled it "Applevill" once? He was brought back into the conversation when the other two started raising their voices.

"We are NOT going to do that. That is ridiculous!"

"You'll do that or the job will NOT be approved!"

This went back and forth for a while until Norman figured out that Chowdahead wanted the pipe size increased from 24-inch diameter to 27-inch diameter.

"The downstream pipe is 24-inches. If you put a 27-inch pipe upstream, it will do no good whatsoever. Not to mention that there is a *huge* cost increase to go from 24 to 27."

"The developer's cost is not my concern. The size increase must be done. The 24-inch downstream has no spare capacity. In case of something unforeseen coming up, I want the extra capacity upstream. Hopefully, the City will be making downstream improvements in the future."

"Is it in your five year capital improvements plan?"

"*That* is not your concern. Now, one other thing: This side drain extends 16 feet past the pavement. That brings it to within one foot of the right-of-way. That will be unacceptable for maintenance purposes. I want that reduced to 15 feet."

Ned softened his tone a bit at this point. "Fine, we can do that."

Norman thought he should break in here. "Excuse me, sir," he said to Chowdahead, "but I used 16 feet in order to use two standard pipe lengths and not have to make a pipe cut. Fifteen feet will be more expensive for us than 16 feet, since we'll have to pay for the two pipes *and* for the cutting. Could we reduce that to 14 feet? That would allow us to use a six foot pipe and an eight foot pipe, both standard lengths. I can make the grading work at 14 feet."

Ned nodded approvingly at this suggestion, but Chowdahead did not seem impressed. "Like I said before, your cost is not my concern. It will be 15 feet."

"But, sir, a reduction of one foot in length will only give you two feet between the end of the pipe and the right-of-way, which does not provide much extra room for maintenance. A reduction of one more foot of pipe will be beneficial for maintenance, will cost less for us, and still maintains a proper distance to the edge of the pavement. It seems that all objectives are met if we do that."

"Yeah, how about that, Chowdahead?" Norman cringed at the way Ned said that, almost as if he was using the name as a pejorative.

"If you want to revise your drawings accordingly, *and* submit this as a request in writing, I'll consider it. Now, you will excuse me please, but I have another meeting to go to."

Ned paused to light a cigarette as soon as he exited the building, and looked at his watch.

"Thirty minutes. Not too bad. I don't think I've ever gone that long in a meeting with him without there being a blow-up."

What was that shouting, then, if not a blow-up, was all that Norman could think.

*   *   *   *   *

Six days later, having made changes and corrections and resubmitted the project to the City, Norman found a letter in his mail slot. It was from Chowdahead to Ned Justice, with Ned's handwritten comment, "He caved. Good work." The letter read, in part:

> We agree with your assertion
> that the use of a 14 foot side drain will

result in a superior maintenance situation when contrasted to a 15 foot side drain. Thus, a 14 foot side drain is approved, but not for economic reasons.

The following comments must still be addressed concerning the calculations and drawings before approval can be granted.

1. Numerous misspellings must be corrected.
2. In several places, you have not used a leading 0 before a decimal point (e.g. .5 acres instead of 0.5 acres)
3. Several abbreviations have been used but not defined in the calculations, e.g. cfs, gpm, in., hr.

It was no joke, though it ought to have been, thought Norman. He hoped he wouldn't have too many projects in Appleville.

Chapter 6
GUS Alert

A week after the meeting with the City of Appleville,
Norman received an unexpected e-mail.

> From: Malinda Mays
> To: Distribution
> Re: GUS Alert—GUS Alert—GUS
> Alert
>
> He's in a foul mood today. Stay
> away!

Norman had no idea why he received this e-mail. It went
out to approximately fifty people in the main office, he noticed.
He vaguely knew who Malinda Mays was: the executive
secretary, working for the president and other officers. She was
an attractive woman, in her early thirties he guessed, who
seemed a bit flirtatious any time he saw her. He had already
heard a few rumors about her, but about such women there are
always rumors. He ignored the e-mail, figuring it had been sent
to him by mistake.

The next day, Norman got another GUS alert.

> From: Malinda Mays

To: Distribution
Re: GUS Alert—GUS Alert—GUS
Alert

He's out until noon today. Afterwards,
watch out!

This got Norman curious. A check of the company phone list, organized by first names, revealed no one named Gus. Re-checking the e-mail, he saw that Peter Pan and Joe were also recipients.

"Say, you guys, who is Gus?"

"Oh, are you getting the GUS alert e-mails now?" Peter said. "GUS is Uriah Serpe, Chairman of the company."

"How do you get Gus out of that?"

"His first name is George, but he goes by Uriah, his middle name. His initials are G-U-S. Surely you've met him, haven't you?"

"Yes, but I haven't seen him much. Has he been on vacation or something?"

Joe answered this time. "He was on vacation for a week or two, then went out on a tour of the branch offices. He got back in yesterday. I'm sure he will be coming by to see you before the week is out."

"What's he like?"

Peter responded, "Very excitable. He gets a notion in his head about something, and charges off at 70 miles an hour to get it done. Usually he gets two or three others involved and ruins their day at the same time. Fortunately, his position as CEO keeps him out of production work, so we don't have to deal with him too much any more. It used to be pure hell. He still has his pet clients, however, which he keeps involved with."

"And," Joe said, "he pokes his nose in all Appleville projects, because he wants to make sure those get done right, what with our home office being here."

Norman checked the phone list again, and found the initials GUS after Uriah Serpe's name. "What else can you tell me about him? What does he look like? I don't really remember."

Joe smiled, the first one that Norman remembered ever seeing on his usually surly face. "About sixty years old; white hair; wire-rim glasses. He's built a bit like a fire plug—short, low to the ground, and somewhat stocky. In fact, he can never stand still when there are dogs around."

A GUS Alert came again the next day.

> From: Malinda Mays
> To: Distribution
> Re: GUS Alert—GUS Alert—GUS Alert
>
> He's making a tour of the office today! In a good mood to start, but may not last. Got caught in traffic this morning. All new people look out— he wants to meet you today.

Peter looked up from his computer. "Better get out of here while you can, Norm. He'll probably want to take you to lunch."

Joe added, "Norm, do you know that you have to pay Malinda for sending you the GUS Alerts?"

"Pay her? How?"

"You need to take her to lunch once a year."

"Oh, well, that's not too bad."

"Yeah. Just make sure it's in a public place."

"Hello, Norman! I'm Uriah Serpe."

Norman took his extended hand, which closed in a bear grip. The middle finger on his right hand had a huge bandage on it, covering the two outer knuckles. Norman couldn't help staring at it.

"This?" Uriah said, holding his hand up and pointing the finger at Norman. "I got this from running my hand over the grill of Ned Justice's new SUV. Picked up a metal splinter from it. Well, how it is going for you at I.C.E.? Sorry I haven't been by before now."

Uriah's every word seemed exaggerated, sort of like Yosemite Sam in the cartoons. Ned recognized him as having been in his interview. He had asked a couple of good questions, but had left early when he was paged.

"It's going fairly well, sir," was his lame reply. Despite the GUS Alerts and the warnings of Peter and Joe, he did not feel prepared for this meeting.

"Great. Listen, I understand Ned has you working on a couple of interesting projects. One of them is here in Appleville, isn't it?"

"Yes, a storm sewer extension project. We submitted it to the City, but it was rejected. I've been making changes, and we should be ready to resubmit in a day or two."

"Hah! Chowdahead strikes again, huh?" Uriah said with a huge grin. "Listen, I'd like to buy your lunch today, then go drive the project. Have you got time? Great! Come by my office about 11:15 and we'll beat the lunch rush. And what kind of a name is Gutter?"

Norman explained that it was originally Gutierrez, that his great-grandfather had emigrated from Mexico at the turn of the century, making an illegal crossing of the Rio Grande. Light-skinned for a Mexican, he figured he could pass himself off as an Anglo, and so changed the name to Gutter. Serpe grunted in reply.

With that he said a few things to Peter and Joe, and was gone in a hurry.

At 11:05, Nancy, the receptionist, called him. "Norman, Mr. Serpe wants you in the lobby right away."

"Make sure you drive," Joe said without looking up from his computer.

Norman quickly saved his drawing on the computer, during which a page came over the loudspeaker: "J.J. Weast, you have a visitor in the lobby; J.J., come to the lobby."

Good, thought Norman. At last he would lay eyes on the elusive J.J. Weast. He rushed out of the building, across the alley, and to the lobby. Uriah was already there, as was a man in a business suit, probably a salesman. He was seated there, evidently waiting for J.J. Weast.

"Come on, Norman, let's get going." Serpe headed to the front door immediately. Norman wanted to hang back for a minute, but saw that there was no way to do so. He followed Serpe out of the door.

After hamburgers at the local café, they went to Serpe's pick-up. Immediately after starting the engine and pulling out of the parking space, Serpe made a call on the car phone. He made a rolling stop at the first stop sign, almost turned the wrong way on the one-way street, and failed to stay right of center. And all this took place in the first thirty seconds of the trip! On they went to the job site, weaving across two lanes of traffic, failing to use the blinker, stopping in the middle of the road. This was just a fraction of the terror that Norman felt on this fifteen minute drive.

They found the job site and drove back and forth over it. Evidently Serpe had discussed the project with Justice, for he seemed to know a lot about it. He stopped several times in the road, oblivious to traffic ahead and behind, to make a note in his day-timer. By the time they got back to the office, Norman was badly shaken.

*   *   *   *   *

A GUS Alert came again the next day.

> From: Malinda Mays
> To: Distribution
> Re: GUS Alert—GUS Alert—GUS Alert

He's in a good mood today! Tell him
a joke.

Malinda called him at 11:00 o'clock. "Norman, you owe
me lunch. Let's do it today. There's a great bar-b-que place up
north of town that no one ever goes to. There's a nice little
hiking trail in the woods behind it that we can take a walk on
afterwards."

Her voice was very coy, flirtatious. Norman hesitated,
thinking of Joe's warning, and wondering if Joe was being
honest with him. He decided to take no chances. "Lunch sounds
good, but how about we do the Chinese buffet instead of bar-b-
que?"

They met in the lobby at noon. She was dressed in a
skimpy little frock, with a purple paisley pattern, a bit tight and
quite revealing. "Let's take my van," she said, as she put her arm
around his waist and headed for the door. Norman hoped no one
was looking, but he glanced back at Cindy, the receptionist, who
had a big grin on her face and was just picking up the phone.

Chapter 7
Togerther the Great and the Trojan Horse

"Get me Togerther!" thundered Zeus from his throne high atop Mount Olympus. Those present cringed at his outburst, and were also shocked at the command. Togerther was a mere mortal; an engineer with an outstanding reputation for solving problems. But while these lesser gods often interacted with the human world, Zeus was above that—except, of course, for his occasional tryst with a beautiful woman of human birth.

Messengers were sent, and a day later the mortal engineer was ushered into the divine presence. His appearance was in stark contrast to the gods—slender in build, average height, with jet black hair showing the beginning of a receding hairline, and brown eyes that never betrayed his feelings. His attire was straight out of late 20th Century America: dark pants, black wingtips, white shirt with pinstripes and a tie showing cartoon characters. He seemed to have been transported back in time. And his demeanor before the great bespoke confidence—some might mistake it for arrogance—rather than subservience. He approached the throne and extended his right hand and with his left hand reached into his shirt pocket to grasp a business card. "Good morning, Zeus. It is a pleasure to meet you."

Zeus' reaction caused Togerther to realize he had committed a gross error in protocol. What was it? Approaching the throne? Initializing contact? Speaking before being spoken to? All of the above? Not knowing, Togerther backed off and waited for Zeus to take the next step.

"Togerther, we have a real problem that we need help with. You have a reputation as a problem solver. We have a military problem that has remained unsolved for ten years. You have come highly recommended to me, and I think you can possibly help"

"There are no problems, sir," the engineer said confidently, "only opportunities. If we can work out suitable contract terms, I'd like to do a project for you."

"Good god, man. There is no time to negotiate a contract! We need help now!"

"In that case, might I suggest we go with hourly compensation for the study phase and 6 percent of construction cost for the design phase, plus expenses billed at cost plus 10 percent. And I will need one third paid in advance."

An angry look crossed Zeus' face, while all others present in the throne chamber exchanged shocked glances at this mortal who dared to ask that compensation be rendered by the highest god. Zeus glanced at a trusted advisor nearby, who gave an almost imperceptible nod.

"Done," he said. "Now, get to Troy as soon as you can. The Greek army has had the city under siege for ten years, and still have not penetrated its walls or forced it to its knees. I need you to analyze things, and figure out a way to break the stalemate."

Togerther smiled. "Troy, huh? Just the type of situation I like—an engineering solution to a military problem. To whom do I report at Troy?"

"Agamemnon is the general in charge. He will probably have you work with an officer on his staff. Come, mortal, time is being wasted. How quickly can you get to Troy?"

"I can leave immediately, Zeus," Togerther said with a slight bow, "but, there is the small matter of my retainer. And I will need a rental chariot to get to the seaport."

*   *   *   *   *

Togerther arrived at the camp of the Greek army a couple of weeks later. Sentries first stopped him, but upon his showing the safe conduct pass from Zeus, he was escorted to the headquarters of Agamemnon. He was amazed at what he saw. Agamemnon was reclining on a couch, a sumptuous midday meal spread before him, which he and three others were consuming with relish. Several young women, clad in suggestive clothing, were serving the meal. One looked like a woman from Togerther's office, clad in a skimpy little frock, vertical stripes in a seemingly random pattern. After Togerther was announced, it was a full five minutes before Agamemnon recognized his presence.

"So, Mr. Togerther, why does the eminent Zeus send you with such urgency into a war zone?"

Right, a war zone, Togerther thought. *This is the most unwarlike military headquarters imaginable.* "Zeus has retained me to see if I can come up with an engineering solution to break the military stalemate."

Agamemnon, with his dinner companions, laughed uproariously, then anger came to his face. "This is just like a god, to think he knows better than the field commander. Tell you

52

what, Mr. Togerther, I will let you talk with my intelligence officer, Odysseus. I believe that he will be able to convince you that we have done, and are still doing, everything we can."

Togerther found Odysseus at the front line, observing the siege and taking notes. They shook hands after introductions were made, then Togerther explained his mission.

"Agamemnon told me that everything militarily possible is being done, and that Zeus' sending me here is a waste of time. Is that your assessment as well?"

"The war is not yet lost, Mr. Togerther, but things look bleak," Odysseus replied, his voice betraying weariness. "We have not, even after ten years, been able to fully enforce the blockade and cut off supplies to the city. Meanwhile, our army has been here without family, rest, or reinforcement. Our supply organization needs to be totally revamped. Morale among the officers and commanders is unacceptable. Desertions have started to be a factor. If we don't take the city soon, we must either withdraw, else we will cease to be an effective fighting force. If you have any ideas, I will listen."

"Gimme a couple of days to scope out the situation, then we'll meet again."

For two days, Togerther went around and around Troy, watching the tactics of the Greeks and the Trojans and examining the city wall structure from a distance. Three times he found himself in the line of fire, and had to scramble and duck behind rocks to miss enemy arrows. He interviewed some of the officers and soldiers, and observed all facets of the military operation. On the third day he met with Odysseus.

"The way I see it, you have two chances for victory: totally cut-off the city's re-supply by a change in your military effort, or enter and sack the city."

"I don't see what else we can do to cut off supply. We have failed at that for ten years. And I don't think the army can survive the additional time required for that to be effective even if we could accomplish it." Odysseus was downcast.

"Then you have to mount a new offensive and get into the city and defeat them in direct combat."

"But how? These walls are impregnable!"

"Let's set up the decision tree on this. There are three ways to get your men into the city: over the wall, through the wall, or under the wall. Right?"

Odysseus answered quietly, "I never thought of this in those terms."

"Okay. Under the wall means a tunnel. But from my observations, soil conditions are not conducive to such a project. Too much rock, possibly interspersed with weak sand seams, and too large of an expense and construction effort. We could do some sub-surface investigating if you want, but to me it seems like a waste of time and money. Also, the chance of secrecy is small with this solution. Time is also a factor, as it will take some time to get a consultant on board to complete a Phase 1 Environmental Assessment, and possibly an Environmental Impact Statement."

Odysseus looked confused at this, but didn't interrupt the engineer.

"Over the wall means a major assault using ladders at multiple points, probably at night, crossing the killing zone, and opening the troops to considerable enemy retaliation. I'm not a military man, but from what I see this would be quite difficult."

"We have tried that and failed miserably," Odysseus agreed.

"Right. That leaves us with going through the wall, which in turn means through the gate or through the wall itself. From what I can see, there is no way you can breach the wall until the invention of gunpowder and dynamite many centuries from now."

"Dyna what?"

"Oh, sorry. Just forget that, and forget going through the wall. I assume you have tried to break the gate with a battering ram."

"Yes, several times. So far we have been unsuccessful."

"Right. That means you need to get through the gate either with a bluff or as a stowaway. Now, since nothing at all is going through the gate at present, a bluff will not work."

"Nor will a stowaway."

"A stowaway will work as long as you create the right conditions. Here's my suggestion...."

*   *   *   *   *

"Impossible." Agamemnon laughed after listening to Odysseus and Togerther present the plan to build a horse that the Trojans would wheel into the city of their own accord. "Zeus has sure wasted his money on your fee."

Odysseus gave Togerther an 'I told you so' look, then said, "No, it will work. We just have to have the audacity to try it."

"So you propose to construct this…this thing, make it hollow, hide some soldiers in it, leave it in front of the city gate, and they will just pull it inside? It won't work, and I can tell you why."

"Then please do."

"It will be so heavy with the men inside that when the Trojans try to move it, they will figure out what is going on. These are not stupid enemies we have been fighting for ten years."

"We have overcome that, general, sir," Togerther said, "by building the horse of a lightweight, triangle frame, using alternating tension and compression members along the same principles of a geodesic dome, with a thin skin and applying attenuation material to deaden the hollow sound. It will be so light that the Trojans will suspect nothing. Remember, due to the element of surprise, it will require only a few soldiers inside. They can egress the horse at night and open the gate while the Trojans sleep. It's unlikely that the barred door is guarded at night from the inside. If another small contingent of soldiers enters through the open gate, and if they capture a few key officers, the city will capitulate. All you have to do is pretend to admit defeat, roll up the horse with an appropriate message, declaring the horse to be a gift to the better foe, and appear to withdraw your troops. The Trojans will accept your 'gift' of the horse, and will commence the celebration. Your men should catch them either asleep or in a drunken stupor." Togerther smiled when he finished this explanation, pleased that he had been able to work in some military jargon.

"You are mad, I tell you! Such a horse cannot be built, nor will the Trojans accept the ruse of us withdrawing our forces."

Togerther responded, "Actually, sir, not only can it be built with materials at hand, but your combat engineers have been working on it for three days, and have it about fifty percent completed as we speak. In two nights you should be able to enact the plan and gain a tremendous victory before sunrise. As for what the Trojans will believe, from what I see you are barely fighting now. They probably think you have half withdrawn already."

Fire burned in Agamemnon's eyes. "What? Who authorized this construction? I haven't even seen the drawings or specs. Where is your site investigation report? And how dare you insult me, you civilian!"

"I authorized the start of construction, sir," Odysseus replied. "The plan is sound, but I had no hopes that you would recognize its soundness and take the initiative. I must insist that we implement this plan right away."

"What? Mutiny! Guards, seize these two and put them in lock-up!"

Odysseus did not move, but Togerther, being unfamiliar with the dynamics between the commander and the officers, elected to turn and run. He could not outdistance the soldiers, however. Despite a head start, after a minute of sprinting he looked back and saw two soldiers about to grab him.

*　　*　　*　　*　　*

Norman awoke with a start and sat up in bed. He was drenched in sweat, and his legs were quivering as if he had just run a 5K. He looked around and realized he was in the bedroom of his apartment. He saw his digital clock turn from 6:29 to 6:30, and the alarm went off. Only then did he realize he had had a nightmare.

"Where did that come from," he wondered? He then realized that working at I.C.E. Engineering was enough to give anyone nightmares.

Chapter 8
Bubba and the Competition

"Hi Bubba. How ya dooin'?" Tank Luzano said to Norman Gutter as he got out of his car at the municipal parking lot. Norman had not had many dealings with Luzano, one of the owners of I.C.E. A Philipino-American, Luzano was the manager of the Headquarters production office of I.C.E. Tall for a Philipino, he had the barrel chest and bulging arms of a weight lifter. His neck, too, was thick and short, giving the appearance of his head sitting directly on his shoulders. He was legendary for being able to bring in business to the company, as well as for getting the most out of people. Peter Pan and Joe had many stories to tell about Tank, especially of his drinking days. It was said that he could drink even Ned Justice under the table, no small feat. The two had been at odds with each other when Tank first joined the firm, till a drinking party at a lakeside cabin had resulted in some unspoken event, something that both of them participated in. They became good friends after that, and stayed together on business trips.

"I'm doing fine, Mr. Luzano," Norman said as they walked to the building. Norman found it difficult to keep up with the older man's rapid pace.

"Don't call me mister. Leave that for Serpe. 'Gutter,' huh? What kind of a last name is that?"

"Originally Slavic: Guttecic. My great-grandfather fled from Serbia at the outbreak of World War 1. He entered the US, intending to go to his uncle's house in Springfield, Massachusetts, but someone put him and his family on a train to Springfield Ohio. It was a community with few Eastern Europeans, so he changed the name to Gutter to blend in better."

Luzano grunted. "Say, Bubba, are you doing anything for lunch today?"

Luzano's accent was clearly foreign, though he obviously was attempting to have his speech be fully American. "I have no specific plans."

"Great! Let's you and me go to the Engineers Club luncheon meeting down in Olneyboro today. Come by my office about 11:00 or so. I'll have Malinda call for reservations."

Norman and Tank parted at the door, Tank going to "Executive Row" and Norman to the Annex across the alley. Luzano seemed like a nice man, someone you could be friends with outside of work. Once at his work area, he asked Peter Pan about his name.

"His first name is Tranquilino. That was shortened to Trank, and later to Tank. It kind of fits him, don't you think? With that build of his he looks like a tank as he moves about. And his effectiveness at doing his job makes him seem to have the engineering equivalent of the firepower of a tank." Peter's words revealed admiration for the man.

The forty minute drive to the luncheon was relatively uneventful. Tank talked about the office, the local college football and basketball teams, and the local engineering competition. "You'll get to meet some of them today. You'll soon see that they are mostly rejects, and not really any competition at all." The ringing cell phone interrupted them, as Tank began a conversation that continued all the way to the banquet room at a downtown hotel in Olneyboro.

Once inside, they went straight to the buffet line. Tank piled two plates high with salad and meats and vegetables, enough food to cause Norman to nap all afternoon. They found a table with two seats available and, after introducing themselves to the others there, began to eat. Tank kept up a steady stream of conversation while devouring his food in large gulps, seeming not to chew. *How can anyone talk and swallow at the same time?* Norman wondered. And those gestures of his! It seemed he had learned to fling his arms wildly about without losing anything off of his fork. Their table companions were from Olneyboro firms. Luzano had not known them before this lunch. He kept waving to various people across the room. Norman saw Chowdahead, eating alone at a table.

"Norman, see that man in the gray shirt at the next table? That's John Johnson of Sandbox Engineering. He used to work for us. He couldn't hack the long hours, and so started his own firm. He mostly does small subdivision design, and maybe some small developments. It was no loss when he left us." Disdain filled Tank's voice.

There wasn't much for Norman to say to that. Besides, before he could formulate a reply, the older man was on to others.

"Okay. Now over there is George Dunbell, owner of Deathstar Engineering. He used to work for us also. He's a good engineer, but always had run-ins with other departments: Survey,

Accounting, you know. Eventually he got fed up and left. It turned out he had been thinking about that move for some time, for within a week of his leaving he was already in business. He took two of our good clients with him, though we didn't do much to hold them. Now, next to him is Abe Butte. He also used to work for us."

"It seems like everyone in this room used to work for us," Norman said, just starting on his apple pie. "Why does everyone leave I.C.E.?"

"Beats me," Tank said with a shrug of his shoulders, and draining his third glass of ice tea. "I guess we train 'em too good and they split. When Butte went, it was quite messy. He had been quietly planning his move for a while. He had even spoken with several of our clients—the ones he managed I.C.E. projects for—and told them he was leaving and arranged for continuing to do their work when he went out on his own. In fact, he had been staying late at the office and using I.C.E. computers and resources for actually running his own business—while he worked for us. Mr. Serpe discovered that one morning. It seems Butte sent some faxes from our machine to one of our clients that he was servicing as his own client on other jobs. He apparently loaded the fax on the machine late at night, went off to do something else and forgot about it. Serpe found it the next morning."

"So what happened?"

"We confronted Butte when he came in the next day, then fired him on the spot. He opened his firm officially that same afternoon."

"What's the name of his firm?" Norman asked.

62

"Hillbilly Engineering. They operate out of Appleville, just like Sandbox and Deathstar." Luzano's scorn for these firms showed in his tone and body language.

"So this is our competition, huh?"

"Yes, for small projects with private clients. They're also getting some municipal work, from Appleville and neighboring cities. I don't know why Chowdahead puts up with them. They have low overhead and rates, and it's difficult to get our prices down to their level and still make money."

He was interrupted when the program started. The speaker turned out to be George Dunbell of Deathstar. He talked about issues related to wastewater treatment regulations for specific industries. Norman thought that he sounded knowledgeable and spoke well, and also handled the question and answer period quite well. After the meeting, Norman wanted to go up to introduce himself to Dunbell, but Luzano said he had to leave.

"I have to get back and discuss something with J. J. Weast. I wanted to do it this morning, but somehow we missed each other."

*   *   *   *   *

Two days later, Norman received an unexpected call.

"Hi Norm. This is Abe Butte from Hillbilly Engineering. Have you got a second?"

"Certainly, Mr. Butte," Norman replied. "What can I do for you?"

"I'm designing a strip center right next to the commercial offices that I.C.E. is designing in Appleville. Chowdahead said I should talk to you. We need to tie into the storm sewer you're designing, and I wanted to get some CADD information from you for the project."

"What kind of information?"

"Your design drawings. Any special layering software you have that organizes and manages the layers would help also. Oh, yeah. I could also stand to have copies of your design calculations. I think that if you just increase your pipe diameter by one size, we can avoid storm water detention on our site. That will save our client a bunch of money and us a bunch of work."

Norman hesitated. What audacity, he thought, to boldly ask for information that was proprietary in nature. And to expect someone else to add to the expense of their project just so his client could save a buck.

"I can give you copies of whatever we have given to the city for review, but will have to check with my project manager before releasing other information."

Norman could hear a sigh through the phone before Butte spoke, obviously disappointed. "Oh, well, it was worth a try. I've already got copies of your information from the City. I was just hoping you'd be a good guy and save me some time and money. Serpe and Justice will never let you give me anything. But say, how long have you been at I.C.E.?"

"A few months. Why?" Norman bristled at Butte's not-so-veiled assertion that he was not being a "good guy," and that he was under the thumbs of Ned Justice and Uriah Serpe.

Butte's tone switched back to up-beat. "It won't be long before you'll be wanting to leave that Mickey Mouse outfit and work for a real engineering firm. How about we do lunch and discuss that now? You can't do better than Hillbilly Engineering."

Norman politely declined both the lunch and the suggestion, and quickly hung up the phone. He saw that neither Peter Pan nor Joe had paid any attention to what he had been saying, and so didn't know, from just one side of the conversation, what had been going on. Norman wondered: Do I report this to one of the managers, or just let it go? He decided that he better inform someone.

*   *   *   *   *

"Don't worry about it," Luzano said after Norman told of his conversation with Butte. "He constantly tries to steal our work, and to recruit our staff. I guess I should have warned you. Everyone recognizes his tactics and ignores him. Just do the same."

Norman liked Luzano's style—easy going in his speech and mannerisms, but with an intensity and expressiveness that immediately won you over. Concerning Abe Butte, Norman decided that the next time he talked with him, he would suggest he drop the "e" from his last name.

Chapter 9
The Architect and the Note

A couple of months went by in relative calm. Norman learned that work at I.C.E. consisted of a number of small projects coming in rapid-fire succession. His storm sewer project was quickly over, as was the design of a sewage lift station. He was then assigned to a small residential subdivision, followed by a commercial strip center. He also found himself assigned to observe a construction project, but the tale of that will have to wait for another episode.

Norman was finally assigned to a large project—a new public school in Appleville. I.C.E. served as a subconsultant to the firm Architectural Manners, Inc., a company in the neighboring town. He was assigned to do the stormwater drainage system design. It was his first time to design a drainage system from scratch, and he was unsure of how to go about it. Ned Justice, the principal-in-charge, told him to go see Fred Dowd, one of the senior engineers. "Fred has done more drainage studies and designs than the rest of the company put together," Ned told Norman one day. Dressed in a purple jogging suit with white pinstripes, with the jacket partly unzipped, revealing a sweat-soaked tee shirt, Ned fished a cigarette out of a pack and put it un-lit in his mouth.

"Yep, old Fred's an odd duck, but he's good at what he does. He sits upstairs across the street, behind the survey department."

And Ned was gone. Norman watched him through the window as he lit his cigarette as soon as he got outside the door of the Annex, then sauntered down the street toward the café, stopping to buy a newspaper from the sidewalk box. It was 10:00 a.m., normal time for Ned to take his second break of the day.

Norman went to find Dowd right after lunch. He was at his corner workstation, fast asleep at his desk, leaning back in his oversized chair. Norman stood there briefly observing the area. For sheer messiness, it was rivaled only by Al Foreman's workstation. A few certificates—degrees and licenses—hung on the cubicle walls, each one askew from being level by a different amount. Piles of papers were everywhere, except on the work table which had not a thing on it except Dowd's stockinged-feet. He had two name plates on his desk: one in English that said 'F.A. Dowd,' and one in a language that Norman didn't recognize. Sanskrit, maybe? Two notebooks and one textbook were opened on the work table, and the computer screen had a text screen saver scrolling which read, "Just Get Lost!" After Norman had been there for a couple of minutes, Fred woke up with a start when his elbow slipped off the arm of the chair. He saw Norman immediately.

"Oh, hello. I didn't see you come up," he said, standing and stretching.

"Hello Mr. Dowd. I'm Norman Gutter. Ned Justice suggested I come by and talk with you about a drainage design I have to do."

"That," said Dowd as they shook hands, "was probably the only intelligent thing Ned did all week. Sit down. Call me Fred. Let's look at your project. And what kind of a last name is Gutter?"

Norman explained Gutter was Italian. His great-great-something-grandfather came over on an early steamer. The name was then Gutterglio then, and he was from Bologna. He was married and had a family there. It was discovered, however, that he was romancing a lady from Pisa. He went there often, allegedly on business. His father-in-law found out about it, and he got out of town fast, got to the coast and bought passage on the first boat he could find, and sailed for America. Once here, he saw that not many people (at that time) had Italian surnames, so he decided to change the name to Gutter, hoping it sounded more English. The older man looked amused by the story.

Dowd turned out to be easy going, articulate, and quite organized, despite the appearance of his work area. As they talked, he pulled various references and examples from his shelves, and showed Norman how to prepare the needed calculations. Forty-five minutes passed as if it were a flash, interrupted only twice when Dowd went to get coffee. Remembering Al Foreman's coffee drinking, Norman wondered if messiness and coffee consumption were somehow related. At last Dowd concluded the impromptu meeting.

"Here endeth the first lesson, Norman. This should give you more than enough to get started. Come back any time to see me, or just call." He stood again and stretched.

"Thanks, Fred. You've been very helpful."

"No problem. Have you met anyone from the architect yet?"

"No. There's a project meeting here tomorrow. I imagine they'll be at that."

"Well, it will be an eye-opener for you. Their headman is Horace Manner. For a job like this, I think he'll have Buddy Little doing the work. Horace will show you just why engineers hate architects."

*   *   *   *   *

The following day, Dowd was proved correct. Norman and the I.C.E. team assembled at the appointed time, and the school district people were there, but not the architects. A call came in saying that they were running a bit late. "A bit" turned out to be thirty minutes.

"All right, let's get things started," Horace Manner said, making no apology for their lateness. He had immediately plopped down at the head of the table and taken charge. He wore a neat suit, white shirt, and a plain blue tie, which somewhat hid his battle with the bulge. Not much taller than Uriah Serpe, he spoke with a similar clipped, direct style that irritated from the first hearing. He and Ned Justice traded barbs throughout the meeting, as Manner made several terse statements that seemed designed to provoke an argument. Finally, Ned made an excuse and got up, pulled a cigarette out of the pocket of his sweat

69

soaked tee shirt, and left, his olive-green jogging suit making a swishing sound as he exited the room. Manner didn't seem unpleased when he left.

"So, about drainage for the project, what's been done to date?" Manner asked, not really addressing the remark to anyone in particular. Norman, cursing to himself that Justice had left, was forced to answer.

"I'm assigned to the drainage study, Mr. Manner," He answered somewhat timidly.

"Well, what's been done? Is the system designed yet?"

Norman was shocked at such a question. "Sir, I've only had the project for two days. It's a thirty acre site. The drainage design will take some time, and there is a detailed study required first."

"I'm not interested in your lame excuses," Manner said, his eyes bulging behind thick glasses. "You come to a meeting like this prepared! Buddy, what drainage issues do you have?"

Buddy Little spoke for the first time in the meeting. "The main thing we have to do is to avoid having to detain excess storm water caused by the development. We have no room on the site."

"You hear that, Gutter? No detention."

"But Mr. Manner, the City of Appleville requires detention in these circumstances."

"Boy, you've got an excuse for everything, don't you?" was the architect's curt reply. "Now you listen to me. Just get this thing done. Do what ever you have to do to make the numbers show that detention is not required."

When the meeting ended, Manner strode out like a bucking bronco, and met Ned Justice just approaching the building from the direction of the café. Manner lit into him there on the sidewalk, gesturing broadly back toward the building. Norman, watching this through the lobby windows, could only assume that Manner was talking about him.

*　*　*　*　*

A week later, after fifteen-hour days, including the weekend, Norman had the drainage design done. He had not been able to avoid putting in a detention pond, but Ned Justice had talked to the architect about that. The drainage report, Norman thought, was a triumph for a first effort. The design was a thing of beauty, incorporating both above and below ground conveyances, optimized for least cost and maximum performance. The drawings had every detail needed. He was ready for their afternoon project meeting, and for submittal to the City the following day. He had even talked to Chowdahead about the project, and had incorporated some of his picky changes to facilitate the review. Fred Dowd had proved helpful in several other conversations.

"Let me first say," Manner barked as the meeting began, "that this drainage system is terrible. Why are we using any underground piping? That will drive up the cost. And I thought I said that detention was not to be used. What is this pond here?"

Norman could see that Justice, relaxed and leaning back in his chair, sweat-soaked tee shirt showing beneath his black jogging suit, was not going to answer. Norman did the best he could to defend himself and his design. Manner kept plying him

71

with angry questions, while Justice sat by silently. Suddenly, as if someone had just pulled on the reigns, Manner stopped his attack on the drainage system and began calmly to discuss other aspects of the project. All then went well, right up until the end of the meeting.

"Okay. I think we're ready to submit tomorrow," said Manner. "Oh, by the way. The building footprint has changed slightly. Here are the new prints. Buddy?"

The assistant passed out a drawing to everyone, and gave out several diskettes. Norman didn't see anything different from the last layout.

"What's changed, sir?" he asked the architect.

"We have extended the building 4-inches to the west. There are also some internal changes that don't affect you."

Norman looked at this for perhaps thirty seconds, then said, "But this extension now violates the building setback line."

"But it's just 4-inches," Manner said.

"We still can't violate the setback without a code variance, and we can't get that now. Not at this late date."

"All right, then. Move the stupid building 4-inches eastward then." Manner's manner again had a wild horse character to it.

"But if we move it eastward," Norman protested, with a hopeless glance at the almost slumbering Ned Justice, "that will encroach on the detention pond. We can't move that any because it is up against the property line as it is."

"Good! I never wanted that stinking pond in the first place."

"It will take us a couple of days to work through this problem. Give me a little time and I can probably come up with a solution."

"No! It must be submitted tomorrow. Just move the building and submit it as is. Chowdahead isn't smart enough to tell that it's 4-inches off."

Justice stood up. Norman felt relieved, glad that the senior engineer present would take up the argument. Instead, Justice withdrew a cigarette pack from his pants pocket, took a cigarette, and began to tap it vigorously against the palm of his left hand. He quietly said to Manner, "Don't worry, Horace, we'll get it done." He turned to Norman and said two words: "Handle it!" With that Ned was gone, the unlit cigarette dangling from his mouth.

*   *   *   *   *

Norman spent the night at the office, alone, running countless drainage designs through the computer, drawing them up, only to find that they did not fit on the site without violating some aspect of either the development regulations or the client's design criteria. At 5 a.m. he fell asleep at his desk, but was awake by six and back at work. By the time 8 o'clock rolled around, there was no solution in sight. He had less than three hours before he had to have the project in the reproduction room. Knowing that Justice wouldn't be in yet, and not knowing where else to turn, he thought of Fred Dowd.

"Fred, you've got to help me," said Norman, having run between buildings and barely missed being hit by a car as he dashed across the street. Norman explained the situation.

"Did you double check the soils type?" the older man asked. "Perhaps it drains better than you have assumed."

"Yes. What I assumed is correct."

"What about the run-off factor? Sure you are not being too conservative with that?"

"I'm sure. I used exactly the factor you told me to."

Dowd, constantly sipping hot coffee, asked additional questions of Norman. Finally he shook his head and let out a sigh.

"Okay. I hate to do it, but we have no choice. We'll have to use the note."

Norman was perplexed. "The note? What are you talking about?"

Fred grinned. His thin frame, gaunt face, and balding head made him look much older than his fifty-five years, but his smile gave his countenance a younger look for a moment.

"The note is something I don't like to use. It's a last ditch effort to be utilized only when all else fails, typically in situations where a client or architect makes last minute changes, the impact of which they don't recognize. Here, down at the end of these grading notes on this sheet…" Dowd took a moment to get to the right place, "you add the words, 'GRADE TO DRAIN. SHAPE TO FIT.' That should take care of it for this submittal. You can fix it later."

"Grade to drain, shape to fit?" said Norman. "What does that mean?"

"It tells the contractor that, despite any errors in the design, he has to make it work. Come on; there's no time to waste. Let's get back to your cubicle and get this thing finalized. And we have to track Ned Justice down to put his signature on the drawings. I'll explain more later."

* * * * *

Dowd's solution worked. "The note" was added to the drawings. Ned signed them without looking, or even asking how the problem was worked out. The drawings were submitted to both Architectural Manners and the City of Appleville. As predicted, neither Chowdahead nor Horace Manner took note of "the note," and the project sped on to approval. Unfortunately, as Norman would later realize, there was no opportunity to correct the problem and remove "the note" before the project went to construction.

Chapter 10
A Walking Wheel and a 100-foot Tape

In addition to the school project, Norman was assigned to work on a preliminary study of a large commercial project, the expansion of a small warehouse in Appleville into a major facility. His first task was to take basic measurements of the buildings on the site. They had a survey, but it was done by a local survey firm, Proximate Survey, and was known to have errors. The client didn't want to have a resurvey done, so I.C.E. would take certain measurements on site, enough to design from. This was new to him, and he found his education and limited experience to date had not prepared him for dealing with contractors.

"This client is a cheapskate," Ned Justice told him. "We have to watch for scope creep all the time," he said, blowing a smoke ring and unzipping the jacket of his deep red jogging suit, revealing a sweat soaked tee shirt. "Go out there and get all the measurements you can, and hopefully we won't have to go back Get the walking wheel and 100-foot tape from Survey, and use them."

Ned walked toward the café, while Norman went to the job site. He got an idea of what he had to do until rain forced him back to the office. Norman was glad for this, as it allowed him to return to track down the equipment he needed.

Unfortunately, the Survey department had misplaced the walking wheel; it hadn't been seen for several months. As to a 100-foot tape, Norman was told in no uncertain terms that such an item was archaic, and survey had discarded any of these a long time before. Let him get one through Purchasing, they said.

Norman went by the office of I.C.E.'s purchasing manager, only to find it unoccupied, with the lights out and door closed, signifying that the man was gone for the day. The nameplate on the door was *Y. S. Mahahghongkar*. Norman didn't even try to guess how that might be pronounced. Under the name was a paper clock with the words "I will return at–". The moveable hands were set for 8 a.m. Norman checked his watch; it was 3:30 p.m.

The next morning Norman hurried to find the purchasing manager.

"Hello, sir," said Norman, not wanting to mangle the name. "My name is Norman Gutter."

They shook hands.

"Hello, Gutter. Yukin Stuffet."

"I beg your pardon?" said Norman, shocked at the words spoken by this man. He obviously traced his ethnic background to the Indian subcontinent. Dark skinned, with short dark hair combed forward without a part, he had a neatly trimmed moustache. He was extremely thin through the shoulders and torso, with long arms and legs. The office, Norman could see, was neat to the extreme. The desk had few papers. Catalogues lined the bookshelf, and several were open on the credenza under the window. Framed photographs of scenes of India were hung in a pattern on one wall. Beneath these were several five-drawer, legal sized file cabinets in a row against the wall.

"Yukin Stuffet."

Norman said nothing, maintaining his puzzled look.

"Yukin Stuffet. That is my name—Yukin Stuffet." He spoke with the clipped, precise pronunciation typical of foreign nationals who are trying to master English.

"Oh, I see. Then why does your nameplate say Mah—." Norman hesitated.

"Mahahghongkar. Can you pronounce that?" Norman shook his head. "Neither can anyone else in this office. So I use my given names instead of my family name. What can I do for you, Gutter?"

Norman recovered quickly. "Yes, I need a walking wheel and 100-foot tape. I wanted to get started on purchasing them, and it needs to be expedited."

"Fine, Gutter. Here is the form you need to fill out."

Norman scanned the paper, which contained the title, "Pre-Approval for Potential Purchase." The information required consisted of: item title, item description, and six signature lines.

"OK, I'm not sure what I have here. Is this a purchase order form?"

"No, this is the form that establishes the description of what needs to be purchased."

"Why does it take a form to describe an item?"

"You would be surprised at how people fail to accurately describe what they want, and how the wrong item can be purchased as a result. This happened not too long ago. That is why I instituted this procedure, with approval of corporate management, of course."

"But I need these items for work on a job site *now*," said Norman. "I have no time for such forms."

"I appreciate your problem, but I am charged with making the financial resources of I.C.E. go as far as possible. You can help expedite this by making your description in detail and then walking the form to the various people who have to sign it. What did you say was needed?"

Norman repeated it, and in response Stuffet simply handed him a second copy of the form, then picked up his ringing phone.

"Yukin Stuffet."

Norman backed out of the office with the two sheets.

Back at his desk, Norman studied the form. It appeared easy enough, though a total waste of time. Both Peter Pan and Joe were out of the office that week, so he had no one to discuss this procedure with. He looked again at the signature lines.

_____	Associate _____	Date
_____	Project Manager _____	Date
_____	Department Head _____	Date
_____	Regional Manager _____	Date
_____	Accounting Manager _____	Date
_____	Purchasing Manager _____	Date

Why did he need his department head to sign this? Why the regional manager, for crying out loud? And Accounting? He dialed the extension on the form.

"Yukin Stuffet," was the curt greeting.

"Yukin, Norman Gutter here. Say, what is the purpose of all these signatures on a form that does nothing but describe an item?"

"An accurate description of an item is the vital first step in the purchasing process," Stuffet said. So precise was the reply, Norman was sure Stuffet was reading off a sheet, or that he had memorized this. He could see him, standing at his desk, waving a finger at him as he spoke. "If the department head and project manager agree that the description is accurate, then we can be sure that the correct item is purchased. The regional manager's signature is just for confirmation. Remember, we had a situation once, not long ago, when a wrong item was purchased due to an inaccurate description, and corporate money was wasted."

"But why must Accounting sign off on it?"

"This way, they will be well informed before the check request arrives at their desk. It's only one more signature. Oh, by the by, Accounting reassigned duties since I had those forms printed. Instead of the manager, J.J. Weast now needs to sign the form."

Norman dutifully wrote his descriptions, one per form, then made the rounds. The first stop was Ned Justice, who for once was in his office. He was seated at his desk, phone to his ear, not speaking. An unlit cigarette dangled from his mouth. When he saw Norman with papers in his hand, he said nothing and reached to receive the papers, in the process rustling the sleeve of his black jogging suit with green shoulder stripes. Ned signed the two forms without reading them. At the same time he started to speak into the phone, the cigarette falling on to his sweat-soaked tee shirt.

The signatures of the department head and regional manager went smoothly. Unfortunately, when Norman got to the accounting office, J.J. Weast was nowhere to be found.

"Oh, J.J. is at the Appleville high school, participating in a career development day," the Accounting Department manager said. "I can sign those in J.J.'s absence." And she did.

Norman rushed the forms across the hall to Purchasing, where Mahahghongkar looked them over.

"Look at this. Justice signed on the wrong line. Did he even look at these first?" He didn't wait for Norman to reply, but dialed an extension.

"Justice, Yukin Stuffet," he spoke tersely into the phone. "Listen, about these forms that Gutter gave you for pre-approval of a purchase, next time read them first, and sign on the correct line, please." He hung up, not waiting for a reply. "Fine, Gutter. I will get the ball rolling on this. You say these are urgent items that need expediting?"

To Norman's nod, the man handed him a form, titled, "Request to Expedite Purchase." Norman said nothing, but merely turned and left with the new hurdle, which included seven signature lines, in his hand.

*　　*　　*　　*　　*

What proceeded, over the next three days, was a nightmare to rival his hazing and his Togerther dream. Obtaining approval from seven people to expedite the purchase of the walking wheel and 100-foot tape, Norman then had to sign off on photocopies of the catalogue pages of the items. Stuffet had said, "Identification of the item to be purchased, from specific manufacturer's data, is the second vital step in the purchasing process." An explanation of how an item had recently been erroneously purchased, wasting corporate financial resources, ensued. A day later, a purchasing order came to his desk. Attached to it were: the catalogue cuts with Norman's signature, the "Pre-Approval for Potential Purchase" forms (which included Yukin Stuffet's handwritten explanation of Ned Justice's incorrect placement of his signature), and the "Request to Expedite Purchase" form. As instructed by a sticky note, Norman walked this through the office, obtaining six signatures. Again, the Accounting Department manager signed for the missing J.J. Weast.

The next day, Norman received a call.

"Gutter, Yukin Stuffet."

"Yes?"

"If you don't mind, could you come by my office. I failed to attach to the purchase order a form that must be signed."

The missing form turned out to be a "Large Purchase Bid Waiver." Corporate rules instituted by Mahahghongkar, after "a recent erroneous purchase," required this form whenever "the request is for over $125.00, or for two or more items, total amount over $150.00, with one of the items over $100.00." Signatures of three corporate officers were required. As Gutter showed his displeasure at this, Mahahghongkar said, "It's only one more form."

Later the same day, Norman found a sealed envelope in his mail slot. Inside was a "Purchase Request Denied" form. Norman ran to find the thin man who was making his life a misery.

"Stuffet, what is going on here? Why was this purchase order denied?"

"Sorry, Gutter, but a check of the inventory shows we already have a walking wheel and six 100-foot tape measures owned by the company. I cannot justify squandering corporate financial resources on the purchase of duplicate items. Use ones that we have."

"But Survey says they aren't available."

"Why are they not available?"

"Well, the walking wheel was lost, and they discarded the tape measures since they now use electronic measurement equipment."

"Lost the walking wheel? Fine, we can replace that. Just…" he said, standing and reaching to the cubbyholes behind him, "get this 'Request to Replace Lost Equipment' form filled out and signed. Now, when you say the tape measures were discarded, were they worn out?"

"I don't know."

"Well, were they damaged? Broken? Or stolen? Or lost?"

"I don't know!" Norman almost screamed the words.

"See here, Gutter, I just enforce rules established by corporate management. This is not my fault. And I can guess that the tape measures were discarded right to the surveyors' garages, a clear case of corporate shrinkage to be investigated. There are, however, two ways we could still order the tape measure. We *can* purchase duplicate equipment, if you get this form filled out." He handed Norman a two-page form titled "Approval to Purchase Duplicate Equipment," with five signature lines. "Or," Stuffet said, "corporate management can always overrule me. Just have this 'Management Waiver of Purchasing Manager's Denial' form completed."

As Norman stood there with a form in each hand, looking incredulously from one to the other, the purchasing manager spoke in an irritated voice.

"I thought you were in a hurry, Gutter. Or, you can wait until I.C.E. does its annual capital asset inventory next quarter, at which time the missing items will no doubt be so noted." Then he said as he picked up his ringing phone, eyes fixed on Norman, "Yukin Stuffet."

*　　*　　*　　*　　*

The next day, Norman came in from the job site to see his message light blinking.

"Gutter, Yukin Stuffet. Your purchase is in. I put it in Ned Justice's office. Please sign the 'Receipt of Purchased Item' form that I attached."

Norman quickly deleted the voice mail, rushed to Ned's office, and took the items while Ned was talking on the phone. Back at his desk, he looked at this last form. There were twelve pages attached to it, including the invoice and packing list from Slater Survey Supply Store, which was located less than a half mile from the I.C.E. office. The purchase price had been $152.77, including tax and a $30.00 delivery charge. Norman noted that, had the purchasing manager just gone to pick up the items, the purchase order would not have required the 'Large Item Waver...' whatever it was form. He went back and found Justice, now at the back door to the main building, smoking, this time, a small cigar.

"Ned, just for curiosity's sake, what was that item, 'recently purchased,' that resulted in all these draconian purchasing rules?"

Justice took a long drag on his cigar, dropping hot ash on his sweat soaked tee shirt, his bright yellow jogging suit reflecting the late afternoon sun.

"About, oh, ten years ago, maybe fifteen, I'd say, the Survey Department put in a request for some running boards for a Ford pick-up truck. At that time, purchase requests were handled mostly over the phone. Yukin had just moved to the USA, and, while his English was good, he was not used to our local accent. When the Survey Department Head said, 'A pair of Ford running boards,' Yukin heard, 'Adair floored running boards.' He understood that to be two indoor jogging tracks manufactured by the Adair Corporation, and made the purchase. A semi showed up at our office one day with boxes filled with the parts for the two tracks, and a C.O.D. order for $45,000. The restocking charge turned out to be fifteen percent of that."

Norman shook his head slightly. Six thousand dollars wasted, ten or fifteen years ago, and a decade of forms and procedures developed so that it never happened again. He hoped he would never have to see about another purchase at I.C.E., thought common sense told him he would cross paths many more times with Yukin Stuffet.

Chapter 11
Tales of I.C.E. of Old

"Gutter? What kind of a name is that?"

Uriah Serpe had caught Norman unawares, engaged in deep thought about a project, studying a hydraulics handbook. He evidently forgot that he'd asked that same question before. Serpe spoke in his usual loud, exaggerated style.

"It's originally German, sir," Norman stammered, somewhat surprised at being asked such a direct question in a cavalier manner. "It was originally 'Gütterman,' but my great-grandfather changed when he emigrated here about the time of the First World War."

"German, huh? I never would have figured that. Norman, I just wanted to tell you that there's a trip planned for some continuing education, and I want you to go on it."

"What's it all about? Where's it to? And when?" Norman asked, thinking about the needs of his projects, and some sewer testing that was coming up soon.

"I forget where it is. You can check with Malinda on that. I know we leave a week from Thursday. It is a seminar about A.D.A. requirements. Sooner or later you'll have to design a parking lot or sidewalk that needs to be in compliance, so this will be good for you. The rest of us need it for continuing education credits, so we're going because we have to. See Malinda about this."

With a brief word to Peter Pan and Joe, the short man went bounding down the stairs and back to the main building. He was barely out of earshot when Peter and Joe burst out laughing.

"Didn't you check your GUS alert for today?" Joe got out between guffaws.

Norman did so, and found the following e-mail from Malinda Mays.

GUS Alert – GUS Alert – GUS Alert

Norman Gutter: he'll be heading your way mid-morning. Get out while you can.

Norman decided he would never miss checking for GUS alerts again.

Later that day, Malinda told him that Serpe had decided that he, Norman Gutter, would be the coordinator of the trip.

"I could do it," said Malinda coyly, "but you'd have to pay me. Let's see, maybe a candlelight dinner at my place the Saturday after you get back?" Despite the coolness of the fall day, she was dressed in a skimpy little patterned frock. Norman had a hard time picturing her as the executive administrative assistant.

"No," he said, choosing his words carefully. "Maybe I better handle this myself. After all, Serpe is expecting me to do it."

So Norman became trip coordinator. He got together the list of people going, then arranged for rental cars. He reserved two minivans for the twelve people to ride in. It was only men going on the trip, he noticed. He arranged for motel rooms near the site, and talked with everyone for preferred sleeping assignments in the shared rooms. Lastly, he went to Accounting to get petty cash from J.J. Weast, who was not there. On J.J.'s desk was an envelope with Norman's name on it, and a note: "Norman: sorry to miss you; had to run to school for a parent-teacher conference. J.J."

A last minute change was necessitated when Ned Justice backed out of the trip. Ned had left Norm a voice mail saying he would not be able to go, leaving no explanation as to why except that something 'urgent' had come up. He was to have roomed with Tank Luzano, so Norman figured there would just be one in that room. The departure time for the four-hour drive was 4 p.m. Norman and Malinda went to get the rental vans, and, finding no place to park in front of the office, pulled in spaces around the corner in front of the café. Norman peered through the window and saw Justice inside, alone at a table, clad in a hunter-green jogging suit, jacket draped on the back of an empty chair, a sweat-soaked tee shirt thus revealed. He was smoking a cigarette, drinking coffee, and reading a newspaper. Is this the urgent thing that kept him from going on the trip, Norman thought?

*　　*　　*　　*　　*

Norman found himself in the middle seat of the second van, next to Uriah Serpe. Tank Luzano drove this van, company president Jim Main the other. The trip began as a lively frat brawl, as every one in the van broke out a beer from a case—

including Luzano—and acted inebriated with the first swallow. Tank especially was on a roll.

"We used to have a wild time at the company's summer party," he said, in response to a question by one of the other younger members of the firm. "Ned and I would get drunk. He could usually hold his liquor better than I could, but, let me tell you: Jim Main could drink all of us under the table. We used to go up to Ned's lake cabin two days before the party, just some of us guys. We drank all evening and fished all day—well, anyone who could get out of bed fished all day."

Tank then told story after story about Ned and Jim, and about many others, some of who were still with I.C.E. They were all variations on a theme: so and so got drunk, so and so dared them to do something, and then he did it. Or, so and so was fishing, and such and such happened to him. The story Norman remembered best was on this latter theme.

"Jim Main and I were fishing that Friday," Tank said. "I was still wasted from the night before, but Jim was going fine. We were getting a few nibbles, but no catches. We could see the fish below us as we drifted, but for some reason they weren't biting. Jim was sure it would just be a matter of time, and didn't want to quit. Suddenly Jim blurted out, 'Oh, no, I've got to take a crap.' I was in the back of the boat, facing the rear, as we drifted with the current, and reached to start the motor to head back to shore, but Jim said, 'No! Don't do that. I don't want to miss it when the fish start biting. I'll just hold it.'

"After that, I heard moans and groans. I never did turn around and see how Jim was doing. At last he said, 'Quick! Hand me that knife.' I did so, and I could hear him cutting something, then there was a splash. Then I saw a pair of underwear drifting toward the stern of the boat, sinking from the weight."

All in the van got a kick out of this, and planned what to say to Jim Main when they stopped for dinner. The dinner was a rollicking affair, somewhat embarrassing to Norman. Waitresses were ogled, and flirted with. At one point Tank was staring at a particularly attractive lady at the next table, when she looked up quickly before he could shift his gaze.

"Oh shoot!" he said. "Busted again."

The last two hours to the motel continued much in the same vein as the previous. Tank, driving well despite his alcohol consumption, seemed to be enjoying himself the most. He told how, when he first came to I.C.E., there was a draftman who spent all his time with a surly look and sour disposition.

"My first day there, he was at his seat when I was shown to my desk next to him. I introduced myself and held out my hand. He never looked up, but just said, 'Screw you.' That shocked me, so I said nothing else, and he was silent the whole day. The next day was about the same. I said, 'Good morning,' and he said, 'Screw you,' and nothing more. This went on several days. Finally, in response to his morning greeting, I said, 'Well screw you too!' He looked up and smiled at me, shook my hand, and we were good friends after that."

It was only a matter of time before Tank got back to the summer lake house parties and Jim Main.

"There was one party, man, when things got a bit out of hand. Ned was plastered, and wandered outside toward the boat dock. We were concerned that he would fall into the water, or something, so we all went out after him. Jim brought the case with him, and so we just shifted our drinking from inside to outside. It got pretty rowdy; lots of shouting and drunken singing. We didn't know there were people in the neighboring beach houses, for we'd not been paying attention.

"Someone made a dare for others to jump into the lake naked. It was a cloudy night, with no moon, and it was doubtful that anyone would have been able to see us. Still, no one took up the dare. Finally Jim said, 'Oh, what the heck,' stripped butt-naked, and took a running leap off the dock. He had just left the end when a floodlight hit the dock from the water, and shone right on him. It was a sheriff's boat, coming quietly in response to a complaint from the neighbors and planning to snap a surprise photo. Their timing was incredible, as they caught ole Jim in mid-leap, one leg thrust out ahead of the other. He was arrested for indecent exposure.

"Ned, who had friends in the sheriff's department, got a hold of the photo. Copies appeared on the different company bulletin boards. Jim kept tearing them up, but they kept re-appearing the next day."

*   *   *   *   *

The seminar proved uneventful. Dull speakers spoke about dull subjects—how to design for handicapped access. Norman, like the others, had difficulty staying awake. The trip back was more subdued. Norman again found himself next to Serpe, who fell asleep immediately after dinner. He leaned over so that he was resting against Norman's side, and did not rouse until they got to Appleville. Well, except for one time, that is, when he spoke in his sleep. With eyes closed, he suddenly jerked upright and said, "Yes, yes, yes. I'll buy that indoor soccer team."

It was a memorable trip.

Chapter 12
The Construction Zone

When he was a student at the university, Norman had always tried to imagine what it would be like to be an adult professional on a construction project. His dad worked for the newspaper, as far from construction as you could get. Yet he fancied himself a contractor, and did lots of concrete and remodeling work at relatives' houses. It never seemed to go well, and Norman learned quite a few curse words helping his dad.

So Norman had been overjoyed to be assigned to construction projects. The first one had been relatively uneventful, as everything went smoothly. The second one was in Williams, the next town over from Appleville—a subdivision project that was mostly finished, but which still needed certain finishing touches. Some new sidewalks were cracked, pavement wasn't draining in a couple of areas, and some trenching still needed attention to be properly finished.

Ned Justice gave him the assignment on a Wednesday in September. Norman went to Ned's office, and found him at his clean desk, telephone to his ear, listening to a voice that was so loud that even Norman could hear at the doorway. Ned waved him in and covered the receiver. "This is gonna take five minutes or so."

It took ten, with Justice saying very little. Norman could tell the call was coming close to an end when Ned pulled a cigarette out of his pack and put it unlit in his mouth. Finally he said into the phone, "Yes, yes, Mark, we'll take care of that today. In fact, I'll head out to the site right now."

He laid the phone in the cradle, leaned back, and stared at the ceiling for a moment. Then he pushed back from his desk and stood. His jogging suit had black pants and a mauve-purple-pink jacket with black highlights. It was partly unzipped, revealing a sweat-soaked tee shirt. He looked at Norman and said, "Well, one more fire to put out. I'd get you involved but I need you at that site in Williams. Come on out back and I'll fill you in."

They stood on the sidewalk outside the back door, where Justice smoked and Norman took a few notes on a clipboard.

"Weiner Valley Subdivision has been a troublesome project. The main problem is the contractor, Nuff Construction. He doesn't do such a good job at following the plans. Nor is his workmanship up to snuff. Here's the punch list of items that need to be done." The list was single spaced and took up most of two sheets of paper. Norman could see, though, that many were the same types of problem repeated at different locations. He already had the drawings with those marked on them.

"Be careful about Bubba Nuff. He's a lazy son of a…well, you know what I mean. You just about can't get him out of his pick-up to look at something. He'll try to get you to do his job, won't help you with it, and blame you if it takes too long or costs him money. Figure on fighting him on most things, and don't give in. Stand by whatever conditions you put on him. In the end he'll cave. If you need help making something stick, talk with me and I'll back you up."

With that Justice was off, heading to the café on the square. He met someone at the corner and engaged in some old fashioned hand shaking and backslapping. Norman went back through the building and to gather some things for the work at the site, then back to his desk briefly for some business cards and the project drawings and specifications.

*   *   *   *   *

At the entrance to the subdivision, a sign greeted all visitors.

> Big Subdivision Project
> You are now entering
> The Construction Zone
> Proceed at your own risk.
> Nuff Construction, N.L.C.
> All visitors check in at the job trailer.
> Safety regulations strictly enforced.

Norman looked around. There was no job trailer. Perhaps it had already been removed since the job was close to an end. He enquired of the first construction people he saw, and they directed him to a white pick-up on the other side of the site, under a shade tree. He drove to it and saw a middle-aged man inside, talking on a cell phone. Norman waited in his truck for a quarter hour before approaching the truck after the man put down his phone.

"Hi, I'm Norman Gutter," he said, extending his hand through the open window.

"Klaus Nuff," he replied. His handshake was a bone crusher, from large hands with sausage fat fingers. Nuff was easily three hundred pounds, and seemed to be tall. "Call me Bubba, though. Everyone calls me Bubba."

"Okay. I'm here to check on how you're doing on the punch list. Shall we go over this?"

"Did Ned Justice send you out here? Man, that's one lazy son of a gun. Haven't seen him on a construction site in three years. You say there's a punch list? I thought we were done."

"Not according to the recent inspection. Didn't you receive a copy?" Norman knew he had, for he had seen a transmittal letter sending it to Nuff.

"I don't think so. Let me see that." Norman handed him his copy of the punch list, and Nuff quickly skimmed the two pages. "Well, this is ridiculous. No way is this much stuff not done. Who's responsible for—" He broke off to answer his cell phone.

Norman went to his car, pulled out the roll of drawings, and laid them across the hood. One of the items marked was close to where he was standing, a sewer trench that showed significant subsidence and which hadn't been seeded. He walked the fifty feet to it and could immediately see the problem.

Back at Nuff's pickup, he waited what seemed like a long time for Nuff to get off the phone. Finally he did, and Norman suggested they go see the punch list item close to them. Nuff said sure; Norman started walking, but Nuff started his pickup and drove the fifty feet, having to do a circle so that the driver's side was next to the trench.

"Well, who put this on the punch list? This isn't so bad."

"The specs call for the trench to be slightly mounded up to offset initial settlement," Norman said, "and it has to be grassed. You can either seed it and wait for the grass to establish or sod it. Your choice according to the specs."

"Sure, but don'tcha think that's kind of picky? I mean, so it's a visible trench. You expect every trench to be finished so that no one knows a trench is there? How're you gonna find the sewer when you need to make repairs?"

Norman looked to his right. A manhole just a few feet away from the trench problem left no doubt as to where the sewer was. Plus the pipe had a tracer wire taped to it—he assumed they had put the tracer wire in.

"It's got to be fixed, Mr. Nuff, and there are—"

"Bubba. I said call me Bubba."

"—about ten other trench locations, water, sewer, and storm sewer, that need similar repairs. Shall we go look at those?"

Nuff sighed. He again skimmed the punch list. "Nah, we'll get to 'em. I just think the other guy who was looking over this job was awfully picky."

A late model luxury car pulled up near them, and a man in an expensive looking suit got out and looked in Nuff's direction.

"Listen, Gutter, okay if I take this punch list?"

"We already gave you a copy."

"I don't think so. If you want me to get this done, I'm gonna need a copy."

"Well, okay. You don't seem to have crews out here, other than those sign installers. When do you expect to start on this?"

"Call my closeout foreman." He took one of his business cards and wrote a name and number on it. "He'll be seeing to this work. Now, if you'll excuse me." He released the brake on his pickup. "I'd better go talk with this shyster. Can you believe these guys get $200 an hour? He's costing me a fortune just standing next to that yacht on wheels. Now, if he'd send that babe paralegal from his office, I wouldn't mind paying for her to stay near me longer. Good to meet you Norm."

He eased the pickup the short distance to the other man, making sure the driver's side was exactly where it needed to be. Norman concluded that Ned Justice had not exaggerated, and may in fact have understated, the key characteristics of this man. Norman looked at the business card. It read *Klaus E. Nuff Construction, Completin jobs for 25 years*.

* * * * *

The closeout foreman turned out to be just as unreasonable as Nuff had been. Norman pointed out items from the punch list; the foreman argued each one of them. Norman said the punch list had to be completed. The foreman called the City out to inspect, but the City backed up I.C.E. and said those were valid items to list for correction.

One by one things on the list got done. Norman figured the cost to fix them had to be a lot more than the small incremental cost to have done them right in the first place. In three locations the street had subsided over a crossing trench, above the buried utility. The repair insisted on by the City was to remove the asphalt, excavate the trench, put in good material and compact it, and replace the asphalt. Except the asphalt had to be cut back far enough so that the repair didn't look like an obvious repair.

The foreman became frustrated enough that one day he threw his hands up in the air, shouted some obscenities, and called Nuff to "come and deal with this idiot engineer," and left. Nuff came to the site, drove to several places where punch list items remained to be corrected, then launched into his own diatribe at Norman. As instructed by Ned Justice, Norman stood his ground.

"Mr. Nuff, I'm not asking—"

"I told you to call me Bubba," Nuff said from the cab of his pickup.

"—you to do anything that isn't part of the original contract. All of these issues are a question of workmanship, not site conditions."

"Yeah, but no one holds us to this standard. No one. Not I.C.E., not Hillbilly, not Sandbox, not Deathstar. Heck, even Chowdahead would let us get by with some of this."

Norman had had enough. Rather than use his own obscenities as they ran through his mind, he told Nuff he was going. They had the punch list. When all was finished Nuff should call him and he would come out and re-inspect.

"Yeah, but you haven't told me how you want them corrected. You expect me to figure it out?"

Norman zoomed off in the I.C.E. truck without answering.

*   *   *   *   *

Two days later, Tank Luzano dropped by Norman's desk, bubbling with enthusiasm as always.

"Hey Norm. I hear you're ready for a new assignment."

"I'm not sure. I've got the Weiner Valley Subdivision to do some re-inspections on, but that's not a huge time commitment. I suppose my office workload would allow me to do some other things."

"Ned told me you were done with the Weiner Valley project."

"No, I've still got to check a few things."

"Well, you might want to touch base with him. Meanwhile, I need you to attend a meeting at 2:00 this afternoon about a new project here in Appleville. You'll be the main designer on that."

"Yes sir," Norman said. He followed Luzano out of the building and went to find Justice. As always, it was no easy task. Fifteen minutes of looking, having him paged, and checking out the eating places on the square didn't turn up his normally-absent supervisor. He called and left a voicemail for him, asking what was up in Weiner Valley.

The next day, as he got to the office, Norman had a voice mail from Justice. It had been left late the night before. Justice simply said he himself would finish the Weiner Valley project so that Norman could devote more time to Luzano's new project. Not knowing where to turn, he sought out Fred Dowd. He found the older man leaning back in his chair, stocking feet on his desk, reading a trade magazine.

"Typical Nuff tactic," Dowd said. "Cry, gripe, and moan. Try to bully you into backing down. And when you don't, go over your head and try to get you removed from the project. Looks like he succeeded. Ned's parents sure named him well. Be glad you're beginning to work for some other people here."

Norman wasn't sure what Dowd meant about the name. On the way back to his work station he passed by Executive Row. Serpe's door was closed. Luzano was on the phone, excitedly gesturing as he did. Stuffet was in Minnie Mize's office, an array of forms spread out on her desk, demanding her attention. Justice was gone, the lights out, the desk top as empty as always. Norman looked again at a nametag in the office. "N.O. Justice." Dowd was right: Ned Justice's parents had been prescient.

The Ned Justice Story
by Norman D. Gutter

The commonest phrase ever heard by men:
"Ned Justice, line ten; Ned Justice, line ten."
Of calls to this guy there seem to be plenty.
"Ned Justice, line twenty; Ned Justice, line twenty."

It's said the first time 'ere the day's even begun.
"Ned Justice, line one; Ned Justice, line one."
He makes those clients just sit there and wait.
"Ned Justice, line eight; Ned Justice, line eight."

He won't pick it up—that much is given.
"Ned Justice, line eleven; Ned Justice, line eleven."
Sometimes it sounds like she's starting to whine:
"Ned Justice, line nine; Ned Justice, line nine."

Don't page him for twelve, 'cause he's still on eleven.
"Ned Justice, line seven; Ned Justice, line seven."
But each of those pages may mean extra fee.
"Ned Justice, line three; Ned Justice, line three."

If he'll not pick it up, they'll switch it to Rick.
"Ned Justice, line six; Ned Justice, line six."
Some flimsy excuse he will surely contrive.
"Ned Justice, line five; Ned Justice, line five."

The pages are heard, but he's never seen.

"Ned, line thirteen; Ned, line thirteen."
When they're paging him, they're not paging you.
"Ned Justice, line two; Ned Justice, line two."

Don't page him too late, cause he's out the door.
"Ned Justice, line four; Ned Justice, line four."

Chapter 13
On His Own

Norman's time at I.C.E. passed quickly. Busyness was the key. I.C.E. received a steady stream of new projects through the door, so many in fact that they had to turn down work. Extra hours became regular. The overtime pay was good, until a change in state law, in response to a lawsuit, ended overtime pay for employees in Norman's category.

Winter passed and spring progressed rapidly. He was able to work for all the principles of the company on a variety of projects. To be out from daily contact with Justice was a blessing he couldn't help giving thanks for.

But his time working with Justice wasn't done yet. A few days before Norman's first anniversary with the firm, Justice called and asked him to come to his office. When Norman got there, he was shocked to find Ned actually in his seat at his desk, not on the phone, and with papers spread out on the desk, and Ned doing something with them. An unlit cigarette sat on the edge of the desk. His jogging suit was peach colored, the jacket unzipped, revealing a sweat-soaked tee-shirt.

"Wow, you got here fast," Justice said. "Give me a couple of minutes to sign some things."

He signed what appeared to be letters—without reading them—then three sheets of engineering seals. These were sticky-back sheets, the kind you peel the back off and stick the remaining transparency on something. Norman recognized what Ned was doing. He was signing professional engineering seals to go in absentia on drawings, in lieu of his actually sealing and signing them. Even as a young engineer, Norman was pretty sure there was something unethical about that.

Ned finished signing the sheets, called someone to come pick them up, then said, "Let's head around the corner. I've been at this desk for an hour. I need to stretch."

And have a smoke, Norman thought. Sure enough the cigarette was lit the second Justice was out the door. They walked to the café on the square, where Justice bought coffee for both of them, and they settled at a table.

"We're a little short-handed right now, and I'm going to have you watch a construction site beginning Monday. It's an abandoned manufacturing facility that's being turned into a large office building down in Nepgip. A building expansion is involved, as well as a huge parking lot. They've been doing mass grading this week, and should be ready to begin some deep sewer construction on Monday. While they were working above ground I was able drop by once a day and keep an eye on things. But next week we'll need someone there full time until the sewer is complete, then again when they work on the water and storm sewer. I'll be on a long-planned vacation next week so I can't do it myself. I think you've learned enough to handle this on your own."

"Who's the contractor?"

"Nuff Construction," Ned said as he lit another cigarette. "I hesitated putting you on this because of what happened with the Weiner Valley project, but you're the easiest to break free."

What happened on the Weiner Valley project, Norman thought, was you gave in to one of your buddies, instead of looking out for your client's and the public's interests. He figured this out even with only a few months of experience at the time.

"I live between here and Nepgip," Norman said. "Shall I come into the office each morning to pick up a company truck and do my timesheet?"

"No, no reason to burn the extra time. Plus Nuff will probably start working real early. Just use your own vehicle, and we'll pay mileage. Head straight to the site from home. Get into the office Friday afternoon early enough to turn in your timesheet. Oh, and get some petty cash from Accounting to fill your tank and your stomach while you're out on company business. I'll have the plans and specs to you this afternoon."

"Sure thing. Who's handling petty cash these days? Didn't they switch that to Malinda?"

"No, it's still with J.J. Weast."

*   *   *   *   *

Norman arrived at the office early Monday morning. He packed all that he needed in his car, then was at the Accounting Department before anyone had made it to work. The first lady to arrive, who he had met before, said good morning and unlocked the door. Norman followed her in.

"I'm supposed to see J.J. Weast for some petty cash. I'm to spend the week on a construction site. Ned Justice has okayed it."

"Yes, we have Ned's note about it. I don't know when J.J. will be in, so let me handle that for you and send you on your way."

He got enough money for a couple of tanks of gas and some lunches, then realized he'd forgot his walking wheel and tape in his office. He didn't know if he would need them or not, but decided he'd better have them. Across the alley and back upstairs he went, into the work area he shared with Peter Pan and Joe The Surly, as Norman had nicknamed him behind his back. He saw a commotion, as a new desk and office chair had been moved in. Data was there with a computer work station. They had scooted Norman's desk over to make room for this one.

"What's going on, Data?"

"Oh, hi Norm. New engineer starting today."

I had to wait two weeks for my desk. This guy better be good. "What's his name?"

"Don't know and haven't asked. Minnie will tell me a little later."

The room was already a little crowded with the three of them. He would be bumping chairs with this new guy. Norman grabbed the items he needed and left, heading for a week of being on his own. On the way out Malinda Mays stopped him, then brushed up against him in her black skimpy little frock. She would be in Nepgip today for a seminar, wondered if they could meet up for lunch.

*　　*　　*　　*　　*

Norman arrived at the site about 8:30 a.m., after fighting through heavy traffic. The typical sign greeted him.

Big Building Site
You are now entering
The Construction Zone
Proceed at your own risk.
Nuff Construction, N.L.C.
All visitors check in at the job trailer.
Safety regulations strictly enforced.

He couldn't find a job trailer to check in at. Several dozers, scrapers, trackhoes, loaders, and dump trucks moved slowly across the site, either adding to or taking from several large piles of dirt. The ground was mostly bare for twenty or thirty acres. A few trees had been marked to save, and there was still grass around them. Norman could see, down at the lowest part of the site, a cluster of equipment and strung out pipe. Sewer construction must have begun already.

He parked near the sewer work and went to observe. The foreman was one of Nuff's men he didn't know. The sewer was twenty feet deep at this location. He saw that the contractor was following normal procedures as he understood them. Trench safety being followed. Pipe carefully strung along the route. Survey stakes everywhere on site. The route of the sewer marked on the ground with dashes of white paint. Norman couldn't believe it. A Nuff project that seemed to be going well.

When the trackhoe pulled off the excavation for fueling, Norman took the opportunity to stand at the downstream end of the trench and sight to the distant stake. Three hundred and fifty feet of sewer would take them to the corner of the building expansion, where a manhole would be constructed, and the sewer would turn in a different direction. The pipes just laid were running true to the stake.

Back at his car Norman checked the drawings. The next manhole was supposed to be fifteen off the building. He walked up there and found the survey stake marked with the manhole location and depth. It seemed to match the drawings. He paced the distance to the building: fifteen feet, just as it should be.

But wait, he thought. That manhole is supposed to be fifteen feet away from the *expanded* building, not the existing building. The expansion was thirty feet. If the manhole was built where that stake was, it would be in the middle of the expansion, and the sewer would be underneath it.

He quickly went to the foreman and explained the problem. The foreman said he built it according to the stakes. If the stakes were wrong it wasn't his problem. Norman looked in the trench. He estimated forty feet of sewer was already in the ground, aimed in the wrong direction. None had been backfilled yet, but would be in the next few minutes. He advised the foreman that what he was constructing was unacceptable and would have to be corrected, and that if he continued to build it that would make the problem worse. The foreman laughed and told him to get hold of Bubba Nuff.

Norman did just that. Nuff showed up fifteen minutes later in his white pick-up. He drove so that his driver's side window was right at the trench edge. Norman explained the problem to him. Nuff seemed unconvinced. Norman suggested they walk the route, with the trackhoe out of the way. Nuff turned his pick-up around and drove to the far manhole while Norman walked by the truck. Nuff pulled up just past the stake, to the point where he could see the far end of the sewer trench. He had difficulty maneuvering the truck between the stake and the building.

"See, Mr. Nuff, the—"

"Bubba, remember? You're supposed to call me Bubba."

"Fine. The building is being expanded here. Look where the new building corner will be." Norman walked to where the new building corner would be. It was painted on the ground but not staked. "The manhole is supposed to be way over here." He walked another fifteen feet.

Nuff scratched his head, opened the pick-up door to get out, then thought better and shut it. "Well, if that manhole stake is off, that's the fault of I.C.E. and your I.C.E.-age surveyors."

"Us? We didn't do the construction staking. All we provided was a site benchmark. The contract says you're supposed to do the staking."

Nuff got on his phone and called his office. "You're right for a change, Gutter. We did the surveying. Well, not Nuff Construction. We hired Proximate Survey to do the work. The office is gonna get them out here ASAP. Now, why don't you trot on down to my foreman and ask him to stop work on the sewer."

Norman looked blankly at Nuff. At least he hoped he kept a neutral look. "I can't do that, Bubba. The engineer can't direct the contractor's personnel."

"But I just told you you could."

"No, I'm not going to go there."

Nuff sighed, put his pick-up in gear, and drove the short distance to where his foreman stood watching another stick of pipe go in the ground. The equipment stopped immediately. Workmen came out of the trench, operators hopped off their equipment, and everyone was milling around. Norman went back to his car and tried, without success, to reach Ned Justice.

An hour later a red pick-up pulled up at the excavation. A man got out and had an animated conversation with Nuff. Norman met up with the man at the manhole stake, and learned he was Rod Holder, founder and president of Proximate Survey. They walked over the layout, looked at the drawings, and walked some more. Holder didn't want to believe the problem existed, but Norman convinced him.

"Okay, Gutter, I guess we've got to move the stake." And he yanked the stake out of the ground, counted off ten paces farther from the building, and rammed the stake in the ground then stomped on it with his foot. "Will that be good enough?"

"Only if you're lucky," Norman said.

They argued about it, Norman saying it really needed to be shot in with instruments, and that the cut mark would not be any good now. Holder said he was being awful picky, but in the end agreed.

"I was only kidding that we'd relocate the stake this way."

Was he? Norman didn't want to speculate.

At that point Nuff drove up to them. About the same time the same late model luxury car Norman had seen on the other job site showed up, and the same man in the same expensive suit got out and stood by the car.

"Well, you sure caused us a lot of trouble, Norm." Nuff said this without a trace of jest.

"*I* caused you trouble? I saved you some money is what I did. If I hadn't found that bad stake you would have built the entire sewer and it would have been in the wrong place. Now you only have to move forty or fifty feet instead of over three hundred."

"Move? We're not moving anything. We'll just curve it from the point we're at and get it going in the right direction, joint by joint."

"No, that's not acceptable. You don't curve a gravity sewer pipe. They have to run straight and true to the design grade. You know that."

"This thing is twenty feet deep. What harm is there in curving it gradually? No one's ever gonna know, at least not until they do some maintenance on it."

"The depth is not a factor, plus it's getting shallower real quickly. The City will find out when then run the camera through it at final inspection. Plus the mandrel many not pull through the curved joints. No, it's got to come out and be constructed right.

Nuff swore and gunned the truck to where his "shyster" was standing. They had an animated conversation, with frequent gestures in Norman's directions. They both made calls on their cell phones. Nuff's foreman came up to his boss and received instructions. Another red pick-up showed up on site. A young woman got out and she and Holder began shooting in the manhole stake. Norman went up and advised them they should probably check all the manholes on the sewer run, which Holder said they would do.

Norman's cell phone rang. It was Ned Justice, calling to ask about the controversy. It was no controversy, Norman said. The surveyor hired by Nuff made a mistake and was correcting it. End of story, except for relocating the sewer installed incorrectly.

"Yeah, let's talk about that," Justice said.

"No, let's not." Norman almost couldn't believe he actually said that. "You know very well that you can't bend a gravity sewer. It's lousy construction, the City won't stand for it, and neither should we."

"Yeah, but that's a lot of expense for Nuff."

"So? He can get it from Proximate. It's their mistake. Plus, their foreman had his men put twenty more feet of pipe in the ground *after* I told him about the problem."

"Now don't go getting upset. I'm just looking out for everyone's interest."

"So far as I can tell our job isn't to approve incorrect workmanship. I won't do it. And, according to the drawings, Tank's the engineer of record on this job, so it's really his call. I've got to go check the new stakes. Bye."

He snapped his cell phone shut, then opened it again and reached Fred Dowd. The man sounded sleepy. Norman could imagine him having stocking feet on his desk, catching a nap at the end of the lunch hour. Dowd said he handled the situation exactly right, and that he should stick to his guns.

*   *   *   *   *

That's how it went all week. It was the Weiner Valley project all over again. Nuff's men did shoddy work on the sewer. Or they had the wrong kind of stone to use as pipe bedding. Or they failed to remove large rocks from the excavated material before using it as backfill. Or they failed to shove the pipe joints home properly. Three times they dropped sticks of pipe into the trench. When Norman insisted they be removed from the trench for him to inspect, he found cracks and had the pipes removed from use.

Each of these brought an argument with the foreman. Nuff came to the site. Norman refused to budge. The lawyer showed up within minutes. Justice called the first couple of times, then didn't when he had no success getting Norman to budge. Still, Bubba Nuff had never left his pick-up.

Years later, as Norman would talk about this time, he said the two best things about this week were breaking free of Ned Justice and the surveyor babe that Proximate kept sending to the site to confirm or correct survey stakes. She was a real looker, she was.

And Norman felt very much on his own, and very much empowered.

Chapter 14
Togerther the Great and the Pyramid of Khafre

"Get me Togerther." Pharaoh's words were spoken softly, to an official standing next to him. That official, however, moved quickly, reflecting the urgency of the situation. A building project was in trouble. Pharaoh wanted the problem fixed. The man from the future was said to be a problem solver, familiar with the building trades. Pharaoh's wish was their command.

A week later Together was ushered into Pharaoh Khafre's throne room. As befitting his Twentieth Century workplace habits, he approached the throne and extended his hand. Before he could get there, half a dozen guards rushed between him and their ruler-god. Then Togerther remembered where he was, and that the customs would be different. He took a few steps backwards and waited, standing at attention.

After what seemed like ten minutes, he was announced. "The eminent Togerther the Great, summoned from the future to consult on Pharaoh's monument project."

Pharaoh didn't speak. Instead two men stepped forward from his throne. Based on their clothing and demeanor, Togerther figured they were high officials. He would rather have dealt with the boss man, but maybe this would work.

"Togerther, please state your credentials."

"What? You brought me here all the way from 20st Century America and *now* you want to know my credentials? Credentials related to what?"

"State your credentials relative to a construction project."

"Well, why didn't you say so straight off? I'm a civil engineer, licensed in twelve states. Most of my work is with public infrastructure: roads, water, sewer, drainage, flood control. You name it and I've worked on it. Even have some experience with commercial development projects. I've been doing this nearly twenty years. I plan it, design it, bid it out, and oversee the construction. Whatcha got goin' on?"

The two officials turned toward Pharaoh, who nodded to them. They turned back and addressed the man dressed in such outlandish clothes, so out of place in Egypt.

"The great Khafre, Pharaoh of all Egypt, is to have a monument to his name, suitable to be the temporary holding place of his mortal body while waiting on the trip to heaven. The work has begun, yet it hasn't. Our construction manager, Hoffenpoffenhotep, has reported that Pharaoh's monument, as presently conceived, will be inferior to that of his father, Pharaoh Khufu. This is obviously unacceptable. Khafre's monument must exceed all the other monuments in grandeur, befitting the greatest Pharaoh to ascend to the throne in any dynasty."

Togerther looked at the man sitting on the throne. He was young; maybe not a teenager, and perhaps not even in his early twenties, but he was young. How could he have reigned long enough to justify such statements?

"What exactly is the problem with the monument tomb?"

One of the officials came close to him, and said in a quiet voice, "We will not discuss the details in front of Pharaoh. Go to Giza right away and meet with Hoffenpoffenhotep. He will fill you in on everything. My understanding is there are multiple problems."

"Fine. But I need to have a night in a hotel. I'm dead on my feet, and I don't even want to think about the number of time zones I've been through. I need a day, at least, before I can function at top mental capacity."

* * * * *

Refreshed after a two night stay at a guest room in the palace, with servants tending to his every need, Togerther went to Giza and met the construction superintendent, Hoffenpoffenhotep. Togerther knew that wouldn't work.

"Can I just call you Hoffen, or Poffen? Or what about Harry? Yeah, that sounds good."

The superintendent didn't speak at first. Togerther was sure he had made some kind of faux pas, but jiminy, he couldn't keep saying that name, and no way was he going to write it out in his daily reports.

"So, Harry, tell me exactly what the problems are."

The Egyptian waved his arm and said, "See what Khufu built? How can we possibly exceed the splendor of that?"

The pyramid was big, Togerther agreed. They were almost a half mile from it, and it dominated the landscape. He began to think of the amount of national treasure that must have gone into building it, when the other man continued.

"Khufu spent so much on that tomb that we have little money left in the treasury for building projects. The workers are exhausted. We are recruiting more laborers, but building up a workforce will take time. I have calculated the amount of material it will take to construct a bigger pyramid, and the amount is simply staggering. Our quarry doesn't have that much stone available. We'll have to find a new source. And, we still do not have a firm design on the interior chambers and passages. Even if we had the money and the workers and the stone to begin, we would not be able to get far."

Togerther looked at the massive structure. He knew from history classes, and a trip to the science museum, that it had taken thousands of slaves several decades to build that. "Boy, what I wouldn't give right now for some ready-mix trucks and a concrete pumper." The foreman lowered his eyebrows, but made no reply.

"So the architect hasn't given you the construction drawings yet? What about shop drawings—got any?"

"Shop what?"

"Oh, right, never mind. I suppose the first thing I should do is reconnoiter the site. Then maybe I need to check the calculations." An awful thought came to Togerther. "Er, I didn't bring my calculator with me because the batteries are low. What kind of computing system you got?"

"I had a new abacus delivered just last week."

"Oh, this is going to be harder than I thought."

*　*　*　*　*

It took Togerther longer than he expected to assess the situation. The site was mammoth. The existing pyramid was of a size that exceeded any project he had worked on before. How could they build something grander? And, as he understood it, for less money, in a shorter time, and with a greater scarcity of materials?

He viewed the quarry and confirmed that it would not have enough rock to make a monument larger than Khufu's. He observed the earth moving going on to prepare the site for the placement of two ton blocks, and wished he could have brought a scraper and a couple of D6 dozers with him. Then, when bedrock was reached, oh to have some line drilling equipment and some sticks of dynamite. He couldn't imagine the number of workers it would take to chip that rock away by hand, without as much as a star drill.

But that was not to be, and he needed to come up with something else. He walked to the far end of the site and looked at the incomplete building pad. Beyond it was the great pyramid. Beyond that was the top of the hill, maybe fifty feet higher than he was now, and about thirty feet higher than the existing pyramid. "Why didn't they pick that site?" he said to himself. "They'd be starting so much higher, and could cut back on the materials."

He walked to the opposite end of the big pyramid and sighted to the new building pad. He realized it was even more of a drop than he first thought. He walked across the base of the pyramid to judge the drop from the opposite side, and was amazed at how wide the base was. That got him to thinking. He tried to do some mental calculations, but couldn't remember the formula for the volume of a pyramid.

He ran to the headquarters tent. "Harry, I've got it!"

*　*　*　*　*

Once again in Pharaoh's throne room, Togerther waited to be called on. The superintendent had refused to come with him. He claimed he couldn't leave the job site for that long, but Togerther heard from one of his assistants that he didn't want to appear before Pharaoh to discuss the major change being suggested. Pharaoh had the appearance of being a mild man. He always spoke through surrogates, and maintained a stoic face. But underneath, they said, he could possibly turn out to be meaner than his father had been. Several foremen on the site said it wouldn't take much to push him over the edge. Togerther had replied "Oh, you think he'll go over to the dark side?" to which the foremen had given him puzzled looks.

At last the officials who maintained their vigil next to Pharaoh asked for his report.

"I figured it out, your highness. Actually, it's rather ingenious if I do say so myself."

"Please, make your report, but as briefly as possible."

"Sure. Two changes, small in my mind, would make a big difference in the project. They will save money and time, and will result in a pyramid much grander than Khufu's. Pretty neat, huh?"

"Please, sir," the official said, "Pharaoh doesn't have time for you to explain it all, or for you to wallow in these self-congratulations."

121

"Sure. The two changes I suggest are: move the site to the opposite side of Khufu's pyramid, and steepen the angle of the sides of the pyramid."

No one spoke for what seemed like an eternity. Togerther looked at Pharaoh, whose face changed to a scowl.

"These are not small changes," the same official said. "Sites are sacred ground. You don't just move a pyramid. Plus we have been preparing that site for a year, and all that work will be wasted."

Togerther shook his head. "What makes something sacred: the ground, or the monument on the ground? Let me explain my reasoning. If you move to the higher site, you can build about the same height pyramid, but it will be higher than Khufu's. Higher is grander, no?

"Then, if you steepen the sides, the base will be smaller, true, but think of how much less material you need. Khufu's pyramid has side angles of almost 52 degrees to the horizontal. If you make Khafre's just a little over 53 degrees, you save thousand of tons of material. Then, if you combine this with the higher site, well, I believe you will reduce the amount of stone so much that you may just be able to use your current quarry for the whole project."

The officials came together and spoke quietly near Pharaoh. The great man himself joined in briefly. Togerther couldn't tell from their faces or body language what they were thinking. Finally the men resumed their places on either side of the throne.

"Where is Hoffenpoffenhotep? He should be here with you to make such a radical report."

"Easy for you to say. Harry decided to stay at the job site. I believe he is already implementing some of these suggestions."

At this, Pharaoh bolted out of his throne and stood. He was taller than he seemed when sitting. He opened his mouth to speak, then closed it, then opened it again. Before he could, the official who had been the main spokesman came up to him and spoke quietly, but Pharaoh pushed him aside. He took three steps toward the engineer.

"How *dare* you come into my throne room and insult me and my people that way."

"Insult you?" Togerther was truly puzzled. "How have I insulted you or your staff?"

"You were told that the ground of the pyramid was sacred. Surely Hoffenpoffenhotep told you that. Yet you dare to suggest we move to another site?"

"? Isn't Pharaoh Kafre a god? Why can't he declare the other site to be sacred? Your highness, I'm trying to help you meet all your objectives. That's what a consultant is for. Some sites work, some don't. You want a monument greater than your father built, and you want it faster and cheaper. The grandeur of the tomb will be based on the height. If you build it uphill, it will tower over Khufu's. If you build it with steeper sides, you can do it cheaper. But it will seem to be grander than the other one. Why, several millennia from now all the people of the world will look at those two pyramids and think yours is larger, simply because of the site and an almost imperceptible change in the design."

"Silence! I will not have such impudence in my throne room. Speak to me no more, engineer, for in the day I hear your voice again you will surely die."

"Yeah, right," Togerther said. "Try that one on your grandmother. I'm outta here. It's a good thing I got a forty percent retainer and round trip travel money in advance."

Pharaoh motioned to a man off to the side of the room. He picked up a large mallet and began striking a gong next to him.

Bong, bong, bong, bong.

Military guards began to close in on Togerther. He started to run, dodging and weaving between men who tried to grab him. He twirled like a wide receiver trying to break free from a defensive back.

Bong, bong, bong, bong.

The door to the throne room was only a few yards away. He thought he would make it until the door opened and a new group of guards ran in.

Bong, bong, bong, bong.

*   *   *   *   *

Bong, bong, bong, bong.

Norman bolted upright in bed, disoriented. He tried to twist, but got caught up in sheets and found himself on the floor.

Bong, bong, bong, bong.

Where was that coming from? He realized at last it was the bell of the church across the street, being rung to call the faithful to Sunday morning services.

Oh, wow, he thought. *What a dream.* Strange names. People who won't follow through on what their jobs require.

People dodging the taking responsibility. Was I.C.E. doing that to him?

Episode 15
A Quiet Lunch

She stayed perfectly still. The Destroyers were active that day. She thought she had finally picked out the leader, and targeted him. He mostly stayed in that white, rolling cabin. But finally he got out and began walking her way. He looked kind of old, tall, fat, and slow. Perfect for her purposes. She would stop him, then maybe the others would go away, and she and her parents could rebuild their home.

If the fat Destroyer came a little closer she could make her move. She had trained her entire life for this moment, endless hours of lectures and drills from her teachers, encouragement from her parents, fantasies played out with school girlfriends, and practice of various attack scenarios. *C'mon sucker... just a little to the left* she said to herself.

She felt a presence behind her, a shaking. She dared not look. Her victim wouldn't take too long to be within range, and he was just right for her purposes. Even a quick glance away would destroy her concentration and possibly cause her to miss this incredible opportunity. But all at once the presence behind had moved to the right and was next to her. She was about to look when he spoke.

"Hey babe. What's your name?"

She said nothing. The fat Destroyer was drawing closer, and slowing down. And he had moved to the left. Perfect. It wouldn't be long.

"Him?" Whoever it was next to her gestured at her target. "You goin' for the fat one? Why? There's a skinny, handsome guy beneath us. Younger too."

"Shut up you maggot. I'll get whoever I want."

"Wow! Big talk for a girl. Well, he's stopped, still out of range. Looks like he's gonna talk with the skinny guy, so you can chat with me. What's your name, cutie?"

She turned to look at this arrogant bore who had about ruined her crowning achievement. She was surprised to find he was her kind, and kind of cute himself.

"I'm Maggitick Nuttalliella. You?"

"Maggitick? Can I just call you Maggie? I'm Seamus Argasid, but my friends call me Itchy. I haven't seen you around. You from these parts?"

She knew the name Argasid, even had some a long way back in her ancestry. They were all trouble, her mother had told her. "No, I grew up in a grassy meadow near the top of that hill. When the Destroyers came we all had to skedaddle, and I came here."

"Yeah, they sure have made a mess of things, haven't they?"

"I'm not sure where Mom and Dad are, but hopefully I'll find them some day."

For a moment they looked out on the ugly sight before them. Several units of big machinery of some type sat idle, though all morning they had been moving, eating everything in their paths like a swarm of locusts. Awful, dull-yellow machinery, the kind that belched noxious smoke and made noise enough to turn even a grasshopper deaf. Maggie never took her eyes off the fat Destroyer for very long. He was motionless now, squatting on his big legs, talking with the skinny one and gesturing with his small front legs, that hard yellow thing now removed from his head and in his hand. They were all Destroyers, having sent her family away from their home, and he deserved what he was about to get. But he didn't move, except for his mouth, and little shifts to keep his balance. She might as well talk with Seamus.

"So what are you carrying?"

"Lyme. You?"

"Ehrlichiosis."

"Ooh, impressive sounding. What's that do?"

Hadn't this dufous been to school? "It's an impressive name, but it's not as lethal as Lyme. Does about the same thing, but it's milder. Rarely deadly. Didn't they teach you about that in school?"

"Maybe. I didn't care much for school. Too hard on the brain. I only went because the girls were easy on the eyes."

"Are you ready for your big move?" Maggie was still watching the fat man; still stationary. What did he have to talk about so long with the skinny one?

"Not really. I don't particularly want to die."

"You don't have to die. Haven't you been trained in *infect and drop*?"

"Well, that only works for deer and dogs, not humans."

"It can work with humans, so long as you don't get greedy. Both of my parents infected and dropped."

"Humans?"

"My dad, yeah. Mom got a deer. I was planning for a deer, but the Destroyers have driven them all away, just about the time I was ready to begin my career. I want revenge."

Itchy looked out at the area, then back at Maggie. "I see what you mean about them destroying your territory. That's bad. But you know that infect and drop of humans is a myth, don't you?"

"No, it's not. My dad did it."

"I doubt if he's telling you the truth. When they find you they put you in dark water to kill you. I did get that much from school." Itchy moved a little closer, and his body was just about touching hers. "My plans are to help build up the population. What about it, darlin'? Wanna do what all ticks our age do, and maybe delay your strike until you lay?"

She would have slapped him—if she'd had hands to slap. She hoped her icy stare did the trick. It seemed to, for Itchy backed away a few millimeters. She'd save her thousand eggs for some gentleman.

"So, where you gonna lodge?" Itchy wasn't watching the Destroyers at all, his eyes fixed on her.

"Under the fat rolls of his belly, right under his belt. I can be in and out before he ever feels it." Maggie looked back at the fat man: still squatting.

"You hope. What about that hard, yellow thing on his head? How are you gonna get on him?"

"I'll have to aim for his shoulder, then crawl under his shirt and—"

"Small target to drop on. Get at his head, then work your way down his body till you get in his pants? My kind of girl."

She moved a few millimeters herself, and wondered why she was talking to him. "So when you do this, where are you going to go? The neck?"

"Nah, too sensitive. I'd figure on getting to his privates."

"You animal! Don't talk to me any more!"

*　*　*　*　*

"So, what kind of a name is Gutter?"

Norman was tired of hearing that, and gave his standard answer. "Didn't you ask me before, Mr. Nuff? It's originally Scottish: McGuttery. My great-great-great...well, I don't know how many greats. My ancestors were a clan tracing their heritage from the Dumfrieshire town of Echlefechan. The ancestor who came to America was a stone mason, and a heavy drinker. He went on a three day binge, later claiming he couldn't remember anything from those days. He woke up in the gaol. About a month later, two Scottish ladies both claimed he was the father of their unborn child, resulting from...activities during those drunken nights. The local authorities first locked him up, then exiled him to Ireland. He eventually came to America with a group of Scotch-Irish, arriving just in time to be pressed into service during the Revolutionary War. He was wounded, taking a musket round through his right hand, and joined General Washington's staff as an aide. After the war, he found it painful to write with his wounded hand, and so shortened the name to Gutter."

Nuff seemed not to have heard what he said. "I told you, call me Klaus. Or, because I like you, you can call me Bubba."

Norman decided to use Klaus. He'd known too many Bubbas in his day.

"I like that camp stool you brought with you, Gutter. Never thought of that for a construction site. And you found this shady spot under a tree to eat your lunch."

"I learned this that summer I worked surveying for a paving contractor. Old man Angel taught me a lot."

Again, Nuff seemed not to be listening. "So what about the change in compaction standards? Are we going to get to drop it from 98 to 95 percent? 95 is standard."

"I put it to the project manager, and he said he'd get back with me soon."

"I hope so. We'll be ready to compact the roadbeds in less than a week. And what about those shrubs we talked about? Those are mighty expensive. The substitute we proposed would work just as well."

"I brought that up to the landscape architect. She said she'd research it, but thought the ones specified and shown on the drawings were better."

"Better maybe, but the cost will break me. What's wrong with him, not being willing to work with me?"

"Her," Norman said. "She said you bid to the information on plans."

A red pickup passed by. Nuff looked closely at it, then smiled and waved to the driver.

"Yeah, but everyone allows substitutions." Nuff stood and stretched, watching the red pick-up. "What about that siding substitution I mentioned yesterday?"

Norman stared at him. "Like I told you yesterday, that's a question for the architect. You'll need to ask him."

"Well, I thought you'd be a good guy and make the call for me." He stretched his arms over his head, his hard hat brushing the tree leaves slightly. "I'd better get back to it. Have you seen that GPS babe? Think she had a boob job?"

Norman decided not to answer such a comment.

"I mean, those can't be natural. I don't know if she's any good at surveying or not, but I'll use that company on every job so long as they send her out." He walked toward the red pick-up.

*   *   *   *   *

Maggie and Itchy held on for dear life, as their leaf was jostled by the fat man's yellow hard thing. Itchy reached for her, but she was sliding toward the edge.

"Itchy! Catch me!"

"Catch you? I'm falling too."

Both ticks went over the edge. Maggie could see they were going to land on the ground. But at that moment the skinny guy did his own stretch, leaning back as he did and grabbing his orange hard thing. Maggie and Itchy both landed on his head, right before he clamped the hard thing down over them.

In the darkness, Maggie could tell that Itchy was near her. She waited, but never did adjust to the darkness.

"Great, now what do we do? It's all your fault!"

"My fault? What'd I do?"

She was tired of hearing his voice. "You distracted me with your talking, that's what. If you hadn't been there, once the fat man got up, I could have been ready, maybe even get onto that yellow thing."

"Too smooth. You couldn't have held on."

"I sure could have tried."

She assessed the situation, trying to recall her schooling. Surely this man wasn't going to keep that hard head covering on all day. At some point he would take it off. If she laid low for a while, she could work her way down to some fleshy part. He wasn't the leader of the Destroyers, but he was one of them, so she felt good about infecting him as a target of opportunity. This man didn't have the belly roll the fat man did, but surely she could find somewhere to latch on to.

"Well, I'm not going to waste my time with this one." Itchy started pounding on his scalp.

"Stop it! What are you doing?"

"I want him to take off that hard thing and scratch. We'll get knocked off to the ground, and I can go about my population building plan."

"Don't! I'm here, and this is the guy I'll do. Within two days he'll be infected. In a week he'll barely be able to move. With luck I'll be able to drop off and find another victim, maybe even the fat man again."

"Ooh, vindictive little tick, ain't ya?"

"He's one of the Destroyers. He deserves what he gets. Hey! I said quit that pounding."

Itchy stopped, turned and drew up close to her. "Okay, babe, you want to spend a couple of hours in the dark, waiting him out. And you want me to stop pounding. I have an idea of how to fill the time. After that, I'm out of here. And I suggest you not go for his belly—not much meat there. Better do what I said I'd do."

What a worm, Maggie thought. To be trapped with him, in the dark, for any amount of time, was not her idea of a good time. How long could she fight him off, but how else to get him to stop that pounding? She had to admit, however, that his other idea, about where to infect the Destroyer, had merit, distasteful as it was to her.

To be continued in Volume 2

Made in the USA
Charleston, SC
05 April 2015